BACK TO THE
TOP OF THE WORLD

**"THE SAGA OF PAPIK AND HIS
FAMILY IS TIMELESS, FUNNY,
BEAUTIFULLY TOLD."**
—*Christian Science Monitor*

**"A POWERFUL STORY OF MAN'S
STRUGGLE TO LIVE. . . .** A tough and
sinewy book." —*Chicago Daily News*

"To describe this novel as 'moving' is to den-
igrate it. In fact, it is an experience. In de-
ceptively simple words, Ruesch has written
a small masterpiece." —*Newsday*

Books by Hans Ruesch

Back to the Top of the World *
The Game
The Racer
South of the Heart
The Stealers
Top of the World *

* Published by POCKET BOOKS

**Are there paperbound books you want
.but cannot find in your retail stores?**

You can get any title in print in POCKET BOOK editions. Simply
send retail price, local sales tax, if any, plus 35¢ per book to
cover mailing and handling costs, to:

MAIL SERVICE DEPARTMENT
POCKET BOOKS • A Division of Simon & Schuster, Inc.
1 West 39th Street • New York, New York 10018

Please send check or money order. We cannot be responsible
for cash. *Catalogue sent free on request.*

BACK
TO THE TOP
OF THE WORLD

Hans Ruesch

A KANGAROO BOOK
PUBLISHED BY POCKET BOOKS NEW YORK

BACK TO THE TOP OF THE WORLD

Ballantine edition published 1974

POCKET BOOK edition published March, 1977

This POCKET BOOK edition includes every word contained in
the original, higher-priced edition. It is printed from brand-
new plates made from completely reset, clear, easy-to-read type.
POCKET BOOK editions are published by
POCKET BOOKS,
a division of Simon & Schuster, Inc.,
A GULF+WESTERN COMPANY
630 Fifth Avenue,
New York, N.Y. 10020.
Trademarks registered in the United States
and other countries.

ISBN: 0-671-80929-6.
Library of Congress Catalog Card Number: 72-12172.
This POCKET BOOK edition is published by arrangement
with Ballantine Books, a division of Random House, Inc.
Copyright, ©, 1973, by Hans Ruesch. All rights reserved.
This book, or portions thereof, may not be reproduced by
any means without permission of the publisher: Ballantine
Books, 201 East 50th Street, New York, New York 10022.
Cover illustration by Robert Schulz.

Printed in the U.S.A.

Contents

BACK
TO THE TOP
OF THE WORLD

1

Pregnancy

The first time Vivi had refused to laugh with him, Papik knew that she had conceived, though neither of them knew why pregnancy made the women of their race, like the animals of the wild, fight off the male tooth and nail: that it was to insure the safety of the budding offspring.

And Papik himself had felt more like sleeping than laughing after the polar night had enveloped their igloo built on the sea ice.

When the light of spring, filtering through the circular snow wall, had aroused the couple from their winter torpor, their bodies had burned up all their fat and much of their flesh, the last provisions were gone, and it was necessary to find nourishment in order to survive. But Vivi wasn't thinking of food, and not even of the child that was already stirring in her womb as if impatient to kick down its mother's door.

"A silly woman has cried in her sleep again, dreaming of her baby girl," she said with an apologetic smile as she knelt to help her husband into his boots.

"When the boy is born, you'll forget the girl," Papik told her confidently. The evolutions of the cormorants departing in fall had left no doubt that she would bear a boy this time. "Now somebody will look for food."

"Yes! a little one can't be so long without it."

As soon as Papik had crawled out through the tunnel, chasing the team into the open with clout and shout, his breath turned to steam and he felt the clutch of frost on his eyeballs—the only part he couldn't coat with fur or grease. He lingered briefly on all fours, scanning the boundless tract of tortured ice, forever reshaped by the winds and sea currents, that stretched before him. The promise of spring had already caused the highest peaks to blush. Otherwise the icescape was gray. That was the top of the world. The land of long shadows. Where all is different—men, animals, nature herself. Where the ocean is solid. Only the warm season brings snow; the winter is too cold for any precipitation. The sun sits low when it is high, circling uninterruptedly above the horizon throughout the brief summer. The dogs are man's best enemies. There are flightless birds, mammals that live in water, sea creatures that move on land, and a scattering of humans who crawl into the ice for warmth. The world calls them Eskimo, meaning Eaters of Raw Meat, though they define themselves simply as *Inuit*— The Men.

To let the world know that they are the only real ones.

By the time Papik had hoisted himself up on his feet, his respiration had already frosted his brows and the rim of his parka hood. He spat, and there was the clink of ice hitting ice.

It was not warm.

Erecting their hoarfrosted furs as an added insulation against the biting cold, the huskies were clamoring for food—barking their lungs out, snarling with teeth that had been shattered with stones lest they chew up their harnesses, or whining in the foolish hope of melting their masters' hearts. As soon as Vivi had squeezed out through the tunnel on her swollen belly, she grabbed the stick at the exit and cracked down on them all indiscriminately, sparing only Toctoo, because he was the leader.

After the pack had been persuaded of the necessity of silence, distant sniffs and bellows became audible— seals coming up for air in the holes they kept open in the ice crust all winter long. Papik hadn't been able to locate them in the polar night during the few times he had shaken off his torpor to search for game.

Vivi beamed at him and patted her belly: "The boy is hungry!"

She was beautiful, especially when she smiled—which wasn't nearly often enough lately. Her lively eyes, black as soot, set off the winter pallor of her skin. Fleshy lips, molded by a real artist, and high cheekbones accentuated the Asiatic cast of her face. She was taller and, when not with child, slimmer than most women of the Men.

"Go back inside," Papik ordered, "and keep the dogs quiet, if one is to return before the sun." And he waddled off, pigeon-toed, owing to the boots of ringed seal that reached up to his crotch.

The Glacial Ocean was resonant and rang underfoot as he trod its gray carpet, causing him to feather his steps until his progress was silent.

Seals don't like to mate in the frigid waters, for which no one can blame them, so at the break of spring they start coming out of the sea to scout for a suitable partner. Before reaching the breathing field, Papik spied a familiar shape lying on the ice like a blown-up, tapered blubber sausage. A seal cow, an early riser, had already come out to meet him, so he wouldn't have to wait endlessly over a breathing hole, working the decoy, at the risk of freezing.

All he had to do was to approach her and kill her.

Seals have weak eyes but a fine scent, and Papik was wearing so much blubber on his body that he smelled more like a seal than a man. Before entering his quarry's range of vision, he shed his bearhides that would have frightened her off, and started crawling on all fours in his inner suit of birdskins. Made exclusively of black birds stitched together by women who measure time by seasons instead of hours, it was no match for the cold, but it helped Papik to look like a seal while approaching one.

He no longer felt the cold. From the instant he had spotted the quarry, he had started slobbering. His jaw quivered, his mouth watered.

The seal cow lay between two boltholes, ready to plunge to safety. Exhausted from an endless winter vigil during which she had had to keep the ice crust open in order to breathe, she was now trying to catch up on lost sleep by taking brief naps that lasted no longer than a few heartbeats. In between she craned, exploring the ice for any approaching bear, or she scratched herself with a flipper or inched forward or wriggled a little on her belly.

When her head remained up, pointing at him, Papik knew that he had been spotted and went into his act.

He curtained off his face with his lank black hair and remained flat for a moment, like a napping seal. Then he surveyed the horizon, swaying his head. Holding his arms and harpoon against his trunk and his feet crossed, he inched ahead, wriggling. He stretched his neck and bellowed, then scratched his crotch with a foot.

By the time the glow of the hidden sun had drawn a quarter circle around the horizon, the seal cow appeared thoroughly intrigued by the dark, mysterious stranger, and Papik was within range. But he could not afford to miss. He had to summon all his will power to curb his impatience. Only when he was close enough to look into the seal's beady, attentive eyes did he throw his harpoon, with a burst of violence that he felt in his guts.

Deluding himself that he had secured his quarry.

He had failed to notice the polar bear—man's only serious rival. So had the seal cow, fascinated by her suitor's antics. It was only when she saw the harpoon go up that she bolted for her hole, moving swiftly on her short fins.

But the harpoon was swifter.

As the thong unrolled, the barbed tip slammed into the flesh of her neck. It didn't break her flight, but before she could plunge into the hole the bear's paw slapped out from behind an outcropping ice block, and the seal rolled over and remained motionless, fat belly up. Then the rest of the bear came leisurely shambling out.

It was a large male, lean from hunger and wise with age. Because its black snout could betray its presence on the ice, the wily hunter had whitened it, rubbing it against the sea crust. The bear sat down on its haunches, rested a paw on the stunned seal, and observed the man, who stared back at it in surprise—at them.

The old bounder had taken along its pregnant mate that now emerged from behind the ice block. The two must have been spying the man for some time, chuckling into their beards, waiting to reap the rewards of his efforts.

Papik's hand went to his flint knife, but his fingers were too stiff to pull it, and his knees turned to blubber with fear.

At the same time he realized why all had gone wrong, and was likely to get worse. He didn't have his hunting charms with him. That explained all. To make sure he wouldn't forget them, Vivi had sewn them inside the parka he had discarded. Small wonder that he was now at the bears' mercy. He couldn't outrun them in his present state, and his harpoon was embedded in the seal. And all at once he felt the full brunt of the cold that he had ignored until then—the chill deep in the marrow of his spine. He had a fleeting vision of Vivi, freezing to death with the child in her womb while waiting for her husband's return.

The top of the world is strewn with little igloos that have turned to graves, merging into the icescape.

But the bears were satisfied with their catch. They forgot the man altogether when the seal cow, recovering her senses, began to squirm. With a swipe of its claws, the male slashed open her belly, exposing a white-skinned pup writhing in steaming blubber, with pink eyes in a wrinkled little head. The she-bear lifted the dripping bundle by the scuff of the neck and ambled off to devour it in private.

A poor loser, Papik chose to find fault with the dumb animal that had outsmarted him. Only a downtrodden husband would allow the wife to walk away with the prize morsel! Cold comfort. Especially as Papik gave Vivi the same liberty.

But only when nobody was looking.

Vivi didn't display joy over Papik's return any more than she had shown worry when he left. He must never know how she felt, all alone with the hungry pack in the tunnel and the child in her womb.

And wondering whether he would come back.

With a groan Papik dropped on the snow couch and stared at the low vault above him. To save blubber Vivi had not lit the lamp, for blubber gives more warmth when eaten than lit, and the igloo was misty with the moisture from her skin. With the flintstone and a tinder of mushrooms, she sparked a fire and lit the wick of dried dog droppings. As the blubber in the soapstone lamp began to melt, the little flame grew, eating up the fog and denting the frost.

Tugging with hands and teeth, she succeeded at length in pulling off Papik's frozen boots.

Whenever he was stoked up to the mouth with food, Papik radiated more heat than a lamp and could warm up an igloo all by himself. But now he seemed a heap of cold meat. Vivi lowered her pants and clamped her thighs around his icy feet, holding them where she was hottest and smiling at him. No reaction. Then she licked his toes warm and clean. As he remained unfeeling and motionless, she touched his face and found it hard as bone.

Her smile waned.

She rapped his cheekbones until the frozen blubber broke off like a clay mask. Seeing the white spots of frostbite on his nose, she wrapped her mouth around it, breathing warmth into it, then rubbed it gently with her own.

At long last Papik's nose began to soften, his eyes became lively, and he took a deep breath.

"The funniest thing happened," he mumbled, his jaw stiff as yet.

"A woman was wondering." Reassured, Vivi leaned back.

"Listen to this. A man harpoons a seal. His mouth is already watering as he thinks of the eating. And then what happens?"

"What happens?"

"Two bears take over—and somebody loses not only the seal but also his harpoon! Have you heard anything funnier?"

Vivi probably had, for while Papik was having the time of his life, she could only muster a wan smile.

"So now we'll have to eat one of our dogs!" he went on, convinced that this was getting funnier and funnier. "As if we had dogs to spare!"

The feel of her skin was beginning to arouse him, dispelling the last chilliness from his limbs, and he suggested that she get rid of her pants. Vivi wrinkled her nose. No deal. Instead, she pointed at the little skylight of clear ice in the snow vault, and cried: "The sun!"

Papik and Vivi stood outside the tunnel with freshly greased faces. The only thing that mattered now was not to miss the first ray of the sun that would peek in but briefly on the top of the world in the year's inaugural appearance. Whoever was not ready to welcome it wouldn't be alive to see it disappear in fall. Already between the gray ice fields and the bleeding sky a tiny green dash had appeared, quickly gaining in brilliance and intensity.

Meanwhile the huskies were crowding their masters, reminding them that they were famished—and that it was necessary to slaughter one.

Papik reached for Karipari, but once more the unruliest member of the team refused to cooperate and avoided capture; so he nabbed a bitch that was forever cringing and whining, telling himself that she was unworthy of the others. The coward whimpered abjectly while Papik gave her short shrift with the knife. After skinning the carcass, he carved out only a slice of liver for Vivi and himself, their stomachs being shrunken as yet and dog meat nothing to dream about, and gave the rest to the pack.

The saying that wolf won't eat wolf may be true; but husky eats husky, once the hide is removed.

The dogs had torn off most of the flesh and were

crunching the bones with their blunted teeth when Papik roared in triumph: "The sun!"

"The sun!" echoed Vivi. "That will see our boy!"

The green dash had become a golden, glowing, growing spotlight that spilled over the horizon, tinting the grayness a pale pink and muting the couple. The pinkness spread over the ice, racing toward them, casting very long shadows beyond each ridge and chip, each block and hummock. Papik and Vivi stood motionless, breathing deep, fascinated by the sunny tide, starved for it. Until it splashed over their boots, crept up their suits, enfolded the blubber on their faces in an illusion of warmth.

"The sun!" Papik burst out again, and started shedding all his clothes.

So did Vivi.

She had the firm breasts that had never known any other support but the muscles of hard work, further bolstered by pregnancy. Roaring for joy, Papik grabbed her hands and whirled around with her, to the baying of the scandalized dogs. Papik could dance more gracefully than most polar bears. Everybody said so and no bear had ever denied it.

Abruptly, he stopped the music. Grinning and panting, he gazed for a moment at Vivi's laughter. Then he forced her to the ground, face down, holding her fast by the nape of her neck. She tried wriggling free, melting a lot of ice under her knees, but sensing that for once he wouldn't let her thwart him—without knowing the reason.

Papik knew it.

It was the first time he had seen her laugh since the last spring, when they had killed their little girl.

2

Don't Cry

They had achieved a victory without equal.

In prehistoric times, ragged remnants of some Asian tribe driven out of their territory had won a titanic struggle of adaptation to a region where no men and very few animals were meant to live. But their conquest enslaved them by so taxing all their energies for the needs of survival that it stunted their cultural development, thus preserving their primitive ways unaltered, deep-frozen as it were.

Their struggle is never over; nor is their enslavement. Even if they submit to no man's laws, they cannot evade the dictates of their habitat. Since wildlife flees human crowds, they must live in very small units—one or two hunters with but a single wife—and keep traveling on their sleds of driftwood or frozen meat, pulled by near-wild and forever-famished dogs. And because life's flame burns intensely in the great cold and old age comes quickly, their main ambition, besides the immediate procurement of food, is to raise a son as soon as possible—an additional provider.

Such is the law of survival.

Although they lead the hardest life known to mankind, they are the merriest of all peoples, and thus probably the happiest. Some ascribe it to their vivifying, exclusively carnivorous fare. Others believe that only the laughing kind could triumph over such ordeals. They laugh about everything.

Except the death of a child.

For Papik and Vivi all went well just before it turned bad. At first their sled, built of the bones and frozen meat of the first seal that Papik had finally managed to kill, danced merrily over the Glacial Ocean, on runners freshly iced, sped on by the north wind that seldom relents in spring, and they had to hold on to the uprights not to be thrown off. A larger slice of sun came out at each turn, but the air remained cold and a canopy of fog from the warmth of the bodies hung over team and riders. Nonetheless Papik and Vivi sometimes rode barechested, grinning at the draft of the ride and sucking in the pale rays of the sun through their teeth.

Individually hitched to the sled and spread fanwise behind leader Toctoo, the huskies pulled fast and hard because they were lean and hungry. A low wail from their master caused them at once to change course to the left. A high note, to the right. But if they spotted some animal droppings, they became deaf to orders and blows until they had gobbled their finds; and when Papik or Vivi stopped to squat, the other one had to stand by with raised stick to keep the impatient pack away.

Although the ice was in slow motion all winter long, night time had been comparatively safe, with the very elements stilled by frost. Spring had changed all this. Above, the Air Spirits had become unleashed, while under the ocean's crust, the old Sea Queen began to stir. The huge water masses swung into motion, gathering such momentum that in some spots they blew up the frozen carapace, mashing it with a deafening din to a maze of huge slabs of ice that mounted on top of one

another and tumbled down and tilted up again. Or else
the crust separated, making dark channels that stalled
the sled until the intervening water froze or the shores
united again, forming pressure ridges that were sometimes hard to overcome.

On the ride, with a stone-tipped arrow shot from his
whale-bone bow, Papik slew a blue fox, the only one
that doesn't change its coat in the winter and is easy to
spot on the whiteness. It turned out to be a vixen, and
pregnant, like all females in that season. Papik and Vivi
ate the unborn cubs, which were ready for birth but still
less stringy than the mother; she was axed to pieces for
the team.

Shortly thereafter their guardian angel went astray.

Papik and Vivi were still licking the vixen's blood
from their fingers when the temperature tumbled and
the steady gale broke into flurries that buffeted the dogs
and lifted the sparse, fluffy snow from the Glacial
Ocean in blinding swirls. To make the gusts go away,
Papik spat at them, but they didn't take the hint and
spat right back at him and grew more insolent. The air
turned white, and when the dogs started entangling their
traces, Papik stopped by the first ridge that was catching
the driftsnow he needed to build a shelter.

Bending in the blizzard while carrying the bundle
they would need inside, Vivi stumbled and fell. A pang
like a menstrual cramp caused her to double over. But
she knew that only laughter could be shared; not pain.
So she kept it to herself. The first pang was quickly
done. Then came another. And another.

She was in labor.

Papik was cutting snow blocks in the wind-shadow of
the upset sled when he noticed that the dogs were
crowding Vivi and lapping up the snow at her feet, although she gave them the stick without mercy. Moving

to her aid, he saw that her pants were dripping blood.

"Is the child coming?" he shouted excitedly into her ear, freeing her of the courtship of Karipari with a kick that taught the dog how to fly.

"It is not impossible!" Vivi shouted back.

The dogs were at it again, crazed by the scent of blood, and Papik had to hobble them one by one, imprisoning their front paws in their harnesses, before he could proceed with his work.

"A woman is causing you trouble," Vivi said.

"A man is used to that," Papik replied gallantly. "And it's for our son—his first igloo!"

Vivi didn't answer. She stepped over the bottom rows of snow blocks that Papik had disposed in a circle, went down on her knees, and began unpacking; but soon she gave it up, resting her burning forehead on the ice and shutting her eyes tight.

While erecting around her a shelter for two, barely as wide and lofty as a man is tall, Papik saw Vivi lower her pants over her high boots and, remaining on her knees, hack out a hole in the ice to make room for the head of the coming child. But for the moment, only blood was trickling into the hole.

Papik worked as fast as he could, at the mortal risk of breaking into a sweat. As he kept adding one block to the other in winding, narrowing rows, he lost sight of Vivi doubled up inside. When the igloo was completed and he crawled in through the manhole, he found her reclined on a rug of blood, pressing to her chest a small bundle wrapped in skins.

She was in tears.

In the quietness of the igloo, the rumble of the ocean could be heard underneath the ice, and above, muffled by the thick wall, the sounds of the Air Spirits, howling and shrieking like human voices.

"Don't cry!" Papik enjoined Vivi, but she couldn't stop, and he panicked. "A girl again?" he asked.

She wrinkled her nose in sign of denial, while her tears kept coming, thick and slow like blood.

"It was a boy," she said. "A dead boy."

"Dead?! But he was kicking!"

"He stopped some time ago. A woman didn't want to tell you."

Papik squatted dejectedly on his haunches. "We must have broken some taboo. We will consult an angakok at once. But you mustn't cry!"

"Should a woman laugh?"

"No. But not cry, either. You will get another son."

Vivi wrinkled her nose. "A woman will never laugh again."

"Yes, you will!"

"No. Because a woman doesn't want to lose another child. She feels sick. She's just a dead weight. You take the sled, and allow me to die in peace beside my son."

Papik scowled. "You speak as if a wolverine had bitten you!"

"Why? You got rid of my mother once."

"Your mother was old and sick, always whimpering and complaining. A man did her and everybody a favor by throwing her into the water."

"When your own mother drowned herself, nobody stopped her."

"Naturally. She had already lost most of her teeth, besides her husband. And she didn't want to be a burden to anyone. With you, it's different. Somebody needs you."

Vivi weakly squeezed his hand. "You really do?"

"Of course. Who chews my boots and scrapes my skins? But you must learn not to cry!"

The more he told her, the harder she cried.

"Listen," Papik said. "Hear how a small boy learned not to cry. That was the only rule my father had taught me: 'Don't cry!' Then in an icequake my right arm was caught between two blocks, and my father was preparing to axe it off. My mother caressed my face, and bit her lips so hard that they bled, but she wasn't crying. When my father had sharpened the flint axe and was about to cut off the arm, a boy started weeping. So my father sat beside me and said: 'The more you fight a pain, the stronger it gets. You must invite the pain, welcome it, ask for more, and then you hardly feel it. The trapped foxes and wolverines that chew through their legs to free themselves don't cry. And their teeth hurt more than this axe. Now, whatever an animal can endure, a man can endure.' "

Still crying, Vivi stroked Papik's hand as he went on:

"My father said: 'Somebody who's in pain feels resentful and lonely, as if he were the only one. But it isn't so. The world is full of pain. If it can make you feel less lonely, somebody will keep you company in your pain.' And my father slashed his own forearm so deep that one could see the white tendons before the blood washed over them. 'Don't think your father doesn't feel the pain. He only wants you to be less lonely in yours. But if you don't stop crying at once, we move on without you, and then if you want to go on living you will have to chew through your arm to free yourself, unless some bear does it for you.' So the boy, who had stopped crying in order to listen, told his father to go ahead with the axe."

"And your arm?" asked Vivi, who had stopped crying in order to listen.

"The funniest thing happened," Papik chuckled. "The boy fainted then, probably from fear. When he came to and found his shoulder hurting badly and wrapped in bloody skins, he believed the arm was gone. His parents forgot to tell him that the ice blocks had opened up again just as they had closed—until the wrappings came off and he was surprised to find his arm still there. But meanwhile he had learned never to cry."

"A woman didn't cry when she got her first child, nor this one," Vivi said. "She cried when she lost them."

Papik ran a finger over her eyelids. "Perhaps it's not your fault that it comes so hard to you. You are a water woman—from the south, where the sea melts every summer. But if you want to become the mother of a real man, then you must learn first of all not to cry. Or else how can you teach him?"

He rubbed Vivi's nose with his own, poked her cheeks with it, and snuffed at her face. Suddenly he pulled back in terror, and reminded her that an abode where somebody has died must be fled at once.

"He wasn't a real person yet," Vivi said. "A mother is sure that his shade won't try to hurt us. We can't go out in the blizzard now." And she dropped off to sleep, clutching the bundle against her chest, and Papik remained alone with his terror of the shade.

Which was much stronger than his fear of the old Sea Queen underfoot or the Air Spirits outside.

"Why not?" asked Papik when the gale had lost its breath and they were preparing to leave. "The dogs eat everything we drop. They'll eat us up too someday, or else other animals will."

"A silly mother doesn't wish her son to feed the dogs," Vivi said. "Let him rest quietly in his first and last igloo."

Papik didn't want to argue. Vivi wasn't well. He could scent that her bleeding hadn't stopped.

When all was ready for departure, he sealed off the entrance. The little igloo, now a tomb for a bit of Man who had ceased to live before he was born, seemed part of the icescape; the drifting snow had already altered its shape. Soon the north wind that now blew steadily again would erase it from sight, helping to preserve their dead child in the deep-freeze of the ice.

Perhaps forever.

3

The Host

Some evil spirit was pursuing him. Papik was convinced of it. Likely as not, the ghost of Vivi's mother, whom he had thrown into the sea. It would be just like the old seal cow. It had been a mercy killing, of course, approved by one and all; but the beneficiaries aren't always appreciative.

As Vivi had been lying listlessly on the sled for most of the ride, not talking, not smiling, not complaining, just bleeding slowly, Papik had diagnosed a case of tired stomach and prognosed prompt recovery as soon as she would get enough to eat.

By now the sea crust was no longer thick enough for a man to be buried upright in, but only lying down. So during a rest period of the team, Papik had sawn a circle in the frosting with the shark's jawbone and started fishing.

At least he had tried.

His nose almost skimming the water that had rushed into the hole after the ice had been ladled out, his behind turned to the sky, one hand operating the decoy and the other holding the harpoon poised to strike, he had been waiting for some fish to come up until his knees grew numb and his buttocks tingled; but in vain.

He was determined not to move when he scented roasting blubber, remote but unmistakable. So did the dogs, starting to sniff and howl.

"There is somebody somewhere!" Papik exulted.

He jumped up, hitched the team, and waddled behind the sled, pushing at the handlebars to speed it on. The dogs needed no whip nor other directions than those from their own noses.

They eventually led to a little snow dome crouching under a ridge. Although no dogs announced their arrival, the igloo appeared inhabited; a wisp of smoke rose from its air vent. They stopped at a little distance and stared at the evidence of life with pounding hearts. They hadn't seen other human beings since the preceding summer, when they had come across a sled of the Netchillik tribe.

Where human company is precious, approaches are guarded. Making an effort, Vivi sat up to inspect Papik's appearance. Then she let her hair down, combed it with the fish spine, and pinned it back up in the high turret that distinguishes the polar women and sways when they move. Only when they thought they looked perfect did they order the team to proceed to the tunnel and to voice their presence. They saw a scrap of seal meat attached to the wall of the igloo.

A scraggly face with protruding teeth peeked out of the manhole and inspected the arrivers with furtive eyes under the Mongolic fold. Then the rest of a Man crawled out and got to his feet, followed by his wife.

The Men's is a vast region but a small world, and everybody knows everybody else's family fortunes and misfortunes. When this man introduced himself as Ammahladok, Papik and Vivi knew the woman must be Egurk. And they also knew that in spite of her name, which meant Narrow Belly, there had been a time when she had shared her conjugal affection and duties among three husbands, life in the North being hard and women scarce. Bears had devoured one of the three husbands a few years earlier, taking quite a load off Egurk's back.

Once identities had been established, grins and greetings were exchanged, everybody bowing deeply while shaking hands with the others high above their heads; no easy feat. Whereupon Ammahladok invited the travelers into what he called his squalid, miserable abode.

He had not exaggerated.

Apart from having twin couches, having been built for two husbands, the igloo was like any other, and the arrivers found in it the familiar sights and smells. The circular wall stained with blood . . . the warmth of human bodies . . . the scents of the wick floating in the melting blubber and of urine kept in the ice vessel for washing and tanning hides . . . garments drying on the rack . . . puppies romping among their droppings . . . and the sweet fragrance of decay. . . .

Papik's eyes searched at once for the heap of seal or bear that should be rotting into tenderness behind the soapstone lamp, but to his dismay there wasn't any. Egurk merely filled a stone vessel with snow taken from the drinking block, placed it to melt over the wick, and sat down beside her husband, demurely folding her hands in her lap.

Egurk was no beauty, younger than old but older than young, and her teeth were worn to the gums by the chewing of leatherwear, as might be expected of one who had softened boots and clothes for so many husbands. Her redeeming features were the beaming smile and happy laughter—hallmarks of all the women of the Men.

And also of the Men, for that matter.

Ammahladok was older than his wife, probably nearing forty and the end of his life span. The rigors of ice-bound life had creviced his face and thinned his hair, but he made up for that by wearing an extra long mustache—an unusual feature on the arctic ice, where usually only foreigners and walruses wear mustaches.

"Have you heard the one about Ippi," Papik asked as soon as they were seated, "who ate his own frozen feet to survive?"

"No," said Ammahladok.

"Yes—just now!" Papik exclaimed, and his hosts burst into the Men's brief, harsh guffaws that end as brusquely as they begin. Papik felt encouraged to continue in the same vein.

"And of the police who arrested my father—but since they had no traveling charms they fell into the water and my father had to rescue them?"

"Tell us."

"A man just did!" This gave rise to new hilarity, bolstering Papik's belief that he was an irresistible entertainer.

"Stories about white men are always the funniest," said Ammahladok, wiping the tears from his ears.

"Like the one about old Pohol. Have you heard it?"

His hosts hadn't, unless they only said so out of politeness, and Papik sailed into the best of his repertory. "My father had known several men who had traveled with Pohol's expedition, the most famous among white men. For years, white men had tried to go so far north that they would be looking south any way they turned. Nobody knows how many had died trying, and had eaten each other up to survive—not to mention the ships crushed when the sea froze. They insisted on traveling as in their own lands, carrying from the start all the food and coal they would need. So they all came to grief unless they turned tail in time, as good old Pohol and his company had done before. Until the Men decided to show him how to travel on the ice, feeling sorry for him because he was so old. It seems that for a year all the white men's tribes below the tree line spoke of nothing else—is old Pohol going to reach the center North? They pronounced his name differently, though.* The trip was not easy, even for the accompanying Men, because Pohol and his companions were not strong and did not feel warm most of the time, and the Men had to take on all the white men's unnecessary burdens. Well, they all trekked north until the white men's magic instruments told them that they had finally reached the center North. And what do you think they found there?"

"What?"

"Nothing!" Papik's eyes began flooding with merriment. "Absolutely nothing!"

One thing was sure. If the snow wall didn't disintegrate from the ensuing laughter, inside winds would never bring it down. Even if the igloo was destined to collapse within a very short time.

But from a quite different cause.

Etiquette required that Papik should continue ridiculing white men for another long while or exchange gossip concerning real men, but his stomach demanded that first of all the subject of food should be broached; so he said:

"While fishing, somebody smelled blubber. Otherwise we wouldn't have had the pleasure of meeting you."

Ammahladok replied in style: "The loss would have been ours. How was the fishing?"

Papik frowned. "The fish haven't come out of their winter sleep yet. That's why we followed at once the scent of roasting blubber."

"You came looking for food?"

Papik's gloomy admission that he had arrived with

* Peary.

nothing edible except his sled started his hosts on howls
of hilarity that Ammahladok explained as soon as he
was able to control himself.

For a year now they had been facing starvation, and
the other partner of the household had gone hunting further afield with the few dogs left—barely enough to pull
one man. But by now he was so long overdue that he
must have come to grief. So Ammahladok, unwilling to
slaughter his only two puppies, had burnt the last piece
of blubber to lure some bear. The scrap of meat on the
outside wall was linked to a burglar alarm made of two
bones that would rattle when pulled. It was an old,
proven trick, that enabled the igloo dwellers to spear
themselves a bear through the wall without stepping out
and catching cold. But by now the blubber had all gone
up in smoke, attracting another hungry couple instead of
some bear.

If that wasn't good for a laugh. . . .

Papik readily saw the humor of it; especially when
Ammahladok decided that now they might as well consume the bait themselves, and sent Egurk out to retrieve
it—and the rattle functioned to perfection.

Only Vivi didn't join in the ensuing laughter, but
said: "Pardon a bothersome woman, who would stretch
out for a while."

The others freed a couch for her, and passed around
a skullmug filled with melted snow. Vivi preferred to
munch some ice she scraped from under the floor hides,
and made everybody happy by refusing her share of the
bear bait.

"You must excuse her," Papik said. "Some evil spirits
just gave us a dead son. And before that, a healthy girl."

"How sad," Egurk said.

"A silly woman is of little help to her husband," Vivi
said. "She can't even laugh with him now."

Egurk snickered and glanced at her husband.

"To help her get a healthy boy," Papik said, "we are on our way to consult Siorakidsok, the old angakok who knows how to predict the weather, to cure diseases, and to bring aid to barren women."

"Siorakidsok is much too old to help barren women," Ammahladok said, unleashing new laughter. "And an overall fraud. He wasn't able to render Egurk fruitful."

Egurk added: "Not even while she had three husbands and kept looking at the full moon."

Ammahladok nodded. "Siorakidsok made her swallow magic potions till she threw up and insisted on exploring her with his finger, but all to no avail."

"So we still have no son," Egurk said. And this could well be our last igloo. When it turns to ice, who will have the strength to build a new one?"

Papik felt increasingly depressed; not a fitting state of mind for a Man. But this was the first time he had been invited into an igloo to just a scrap of bear bait and, worse, without being able to humiliate his hosts by forcing upon them an exaggerated share of his own hunt. He brooded until he suddenly went down on all fours, crawled out through the tunnel, and returned waving a length of frozen meat: a crossbar from his sled.

"You can't spare that," Ammahladok said, his eyes bulging.

"Our sled has more crossbars," Papik assured him, and added a little lie: "Besides, a man likes to run with the dogs."

His hosts tried to refuse a gift that circumstances made very valuable, and therefore particularly humiliating; but after Papik had started sucking at the bar himself, it would have been rude for them not to share in it. So the length of frozen meat passed from mouth to mouth, thawing and waning rapidly as appetites awakened.

Even Vivi put in a couple of licks, but mainly to be sociable.

The crossbar stayed momentarily the pangs of hunger and brightened the glow of conviviality in hearts starved for human company. Smiles were wide with the eagerness to please, eyes shone with laughter, and conversation was lively.

Only Vivi did not participate.

When she faced the wall and pulled a hide over her head, indicating her wish to sleep, Ammahladok glanced from his wife to Papik and grinned:

"Life is sad when a wife is sick."

"Very sad," Papik grinned back.

"Very," said Egurk, muffling a giggle.

They kept exchanging grins and glances until Papik, growing impatient but minding his manners, declared:

"Somebody doesn't wish to impose."

"It is no imposition." Ammahladok took his blushing wife by the hand, drew her gently in front of Papik, and exclaimed:

"Be one!"

Laughter is not always grounds for sex, but sex is always grounds for laughter. Papik and Egurk snickered shamefacedly, and Ammahladok repeated:

"A man is sad if his wife can't laugh."

Suddenly Papik had second thoughts, and said: "Somebody can't repay you in kind."

Ammahladok reassured him: "We may meet again. So don't turn down a poor host's worthless offer."

Papik had enough strength of character to forget his pride when Ammahladok, displaying great tact, reached for his bearhides and said:

"A man can hear your dogs fighting. He will see to it."

It was a fact. An uproar of dogs had been audible for

a little while now. Egurk assisted her husband as he put
on his boots and Papik also sped his host's departure by
helping him into his parka.

While Ammahladok crawled out through the tunnel,
Papik glanced at Vivi. She seemed sound asleep; unless
she was pretending, like the well-bred, discreet wife that
she was. He dropped on his knees to seal the entrance
with the block of drinking snow, then turned to Egurk
with an embarrassed grin.

She was tittering behind her hand, her face aflame up
to the hair roots.

In spite of their mutual bashfulness, Papik had been
making good-humored headway with the hostess'when
the muffled voice of Ammahladok resounded in the tunnel and the snowblock that sealed the entrance inched in-
ward, as if someone wanted to gain admittance. Outside,
the huskies sounded wilder than ever, and Papik thought
they were giving Ammahladok trouble, but he couldn't
have cared less at the moment.

He withdrew from Egurk to push the snowplug back
into place and shout that it was not nearly time yet for a
husband to come home. But Ammahladok insisted to
the point of rudeness, at the risk of cooling Papik's ar-
dor and waking up Vivi. Mumbling unintelligibly, he
kept pushing from the outside at the plug that Papik, flat
on his chest and buttocks aloft, was holding steady from
the inside. Until the block crumbled and Ammahladok's
snowpowdered face poked through, eyeball to eyeball
with Papik's.

"Bears are here!" he sputtered, frantically squirming
in. "They are sniffing at my pants!"

He got up and made for his spear, but Papik beat him
to it and shoved him against the wall, thundering:

"Out of my way! Now *you* are *my* guest. . . ."

4

Food

There are many ways to kill a bear and the Men know most of them. But they never know who is going to win, for their weapons are made of driftwood and bone, of flintstone and ivory, and to kill their quarries they must get close enough to look them in the eyes.

Bear is superior to man on many counts: it can walk on two legs, like man, but also on all four, which man cannot do; it surpasses man in strength and endurance; it outswims man in the freezing waters, outruns him on the slick ice with its claws and bristly pads, and can weather the smothering blizzard without shelter. Man has but one advantage over the bear, and it isn't his brains; it's the ten fingers on his hands.

Not even striking out through a hole in the wall when the bear comes ringing at the housedoor is entirely safe. The bear may not collaborate, placing itself in the wrong spot or refusing to hold still, and if it is merely wounded, it can become very annoyed and decide to crush the igloo.

The bears that had belatedly answered Ammahla-dok's call of roasting blubber didn't have to smash his igloo because Papik did it for them. In his impatience to get out, he butted his way through the wall, bringing the vault down and emerging in the open with snow on his head and spear in hand.

The area in front of the igloo, flaming in the sun that had just risen, was a battlefield for the hobbled dogs and four polar bears, one of them still a cub.

Some dogs had broken their bonds. Two lay bleeding. One of these was Toctoo. Still hobbled, with a front paw tucked into the collar, the lead dog had snapped its trace and attacked the attackers. Now it lay with its shank torn open; a shiny whiteness of bone in velvety red. Although breathing its last, Toctoo still found the strength to snarl at the bears with its shattered teeth and to welcome its master with a whine and a wag.

The bears were hungry enough after a lean winter to overcome their natural diffidence of man. The nearest male rose on its hindquarters and, towering over Papik, reached out with its paws, but the spearhead slammed through its mouth and palate and into the brain. Papik twisted away from the thousand pounds that came crashing down with a thud that shook the ice.

This kill was fast and risky. Any deflection of the spear would have made of the victor the victim. Meanwhile another male was beset by dogs that were raging at its hams. Growling, it was striking out with its paws, but even the dogs that had been clawed hung on. Their blunted fangs couldn't pierce the shaggy hide, but they hampered its wearer so that Papik could spear it as well, anticipating Ammahladok who had come out with his axe.

At that point the she-bear broke away from a tug-of-war with snarling Karipari and ambled off. The cub, which had mistaken the battle for a game, romping between the killers and the killed, didn't follow. So the mother came loping back and cuffed it.

Whereafter both left together.

After the bears' scalding blood had been drunk

straight from the tap, the brain was sucked out through a hole drilled into the base of the skull. As appetites awoke and stomachs widened, ever more meat turned to flesh. The bears must have been very hungry, for there were lichens and twigs in their intestines.

During the next few turns of the sun, there was no time for rebuilding the igloo. Vivi, still bleeding, was too weak to work, and the other three were too busy eating and laughing, eating and recounting the details, eating and feeding the team, eating and skinning the kills, eating and scraping the hides, eating and curing the meats.

Nomads must travel light, with scant provisions, and Papik could profit only by the meat that passed through his stomach before departure; so he glutted himself with a will, admiring his naked belly that was spreading in the sunshine. When he was unable to stand on his feet, he stretched out on his back and allowed Egurk to drop tidbits into his gaping mouth.

But the pack was kept on stingy rations; even the puppies. Thus the Polar Men had developed a strain of draft-dogs that, although only a shade weaker than the southern ones, were much smaller and so required far less food.

To replace Toctoo, Papik chose Karipari—a daring decision that was to bear fruit.

In order to build up the self-esteem of the most abused and punished member of the pack, Karipari was admitted on the couch-spread of its mistress, among the mysterious odors of her skin; was fed choice morsels; experienced the masters' caresses on its muzzle instead of their stick on its loins; and was addressed in the low, soft tones of affection.

Until the rebel became an ally.

And Karipari knew its duties without having to be told. It would separate fighting teammates by dashing between them with angry snarls. And the first time it caught one of them gnawing at the sled, it intervened with such zeal that the criminal lost half an ear.

After helping their hosts in rebuilding the igloo, Papik and Vivi parted from them without farewells, for where company is rare, separations are painful and therefore best ignored. When the sled was ready to leave, Ammahladok and Egurk tactfully walked away from it, pretending to be terribly busy.

Papik had humiliated them by leaving with them all the meat he had procured, not to mention the pelts he didn't want. The hosts had taken revenge by giving him their two puppies, to help him replace his losses.

Vivi mused as they drove off: "Egurk is afraid that this is their last igloo."

"It is not impossible," said Papik, cracking the whip.

They traveled in an icy empire on which the sun never set. The red orb of spring had been bled white by its efforts to hoist itself up to stay, and now rode continually above the horizon, rising a little on one side and sinking slightly on the opposite point, and casting slowly circling shadows that were all long and light because the rays were low and weak. But their uninterrupted presence and reverberation on the ice made for such warmth that vapors rose from the ground, partly erasing the horizon, the conical islands and jagged icebergs rising from the seacrust, and bringing on the first snow flurries.

As they moved southward, the sea crust became more hazardous. It split open frequently, and once Karipari had to swerve sharply, lest the ocean engulf them all—team, sled, and riders. Sometimes the north wind lost its breath, and then the air filled with the smells of summer —of distant blossoms and the brine of the open sea.

They traveled without counting the turns of the sun, seeing no man and little wildlife.

Due to the uninterrupted exposure, their faces lost before long the pale yellowness of winter and turned the color of burnished copper. Because it was always day, they never slept, except for occasional little naps. They had stored up sufficient rest during the long night to last them all summer. Now they wanted to put on flesh and store up sunshine for the coming winter.

Since daylight had seeped through the frosting, the fish had come to life and allowed themselves to be lured to the surface and speared in the holes Papik sawed in the ice crust; mainly iridescent, red-bellied trout, and spotted, sun-hued salmon. More important was the seal he bagged by pretending he was one of them. The oily blood and crimson meat eaten between slices of blubber did wonders for Vivi. She began to haul weights again, to scrape hides and chew boots, although neither the wound in her womb nor the one in her heart had entirely healed.

But Papik was sure that a summer's gorging and a capable angakok would take care of that.

Once the strong north wind or some submarine storm separated the crust on which they traveled from the main ice, and for two or three turns of the sun they found themselves adrift on the open ocean on a floe that was smaller than an island but not much, until they hit a coast and moved onto land, where the dwarf vegetation was beginning to push through the melting snow, and the glaciers were thunderously calving the season's first icebergs into the liquefied ocean.

And there they hit the big snag.

5

The Massacre

They had finished eating up their sled and were trying to find their bearings in a region that changed face each year when Vivi called out excitedly that she had sighted a boat.

It was a white men's ship, moving under its own power, sailing close to shore. Someone on board waved and the couple answered, delighted and flattered. The ship lowered a launch then and disembarked three white men.

A fair-haired one who spoke the language of the Men quite intelligibly but wasted no time in kowtows informed Papik that the white men who flew in the sky had sighted a drifting seal patch, and that he would be rewarded handsomely if he would join in the killing. Finding hands was the great problem in a land of wide spaces and few people.

Vivi remembered her father telling her of big whaling vessels arriving from below the tree line every summer, manned by blond devils who invited the Eskimos on board and made them unconscious with firewater or a whack on the head, and when they came around they found themselves on the high seas. It was the only way the vessels' crews could be completed for their whaling expeditions in the dangerous arctic waters.

Those times were gone; so were most whales.

At present the foreigners wanted help for their sealing expeditions. They didn't whack Papik on the head; nowadays it was taboo. But they promised him seals and presents, and accepted taking Vivi on board, and even his dogteam.

Papik accepted the invitation with enthusiasm. But not for the reward. On the contrary. He was eager to show those foreigners how seals were hunted. Like all modest heroes, he craved recognition—both for his heroism and his modesty.

However, each time he had ventured into the treacherous, unpredictable South, Papik had regretted it. The world below the perennial ice seemed to be inhabited mainly by foreigners, who didn't know how to live and did extravagant things. This occurred to him again as soon as the white men's launch headed for the sealing vessel. It was the first time he wasn't sailing on an ice floe but in a wooden boat, and he soon discovered that there was something sinister about it, apart from the danger of drowning. The sea, dotted with icebergs, was choppy, and presently Papik was experiencing the miseries of seasickness, aggravated by the necessity of saving face in front of strangers, concealing his state.

Not to mention the humiliation that Vivi, a mere woman, proved a far better sailor.

Although Papik sat bolt upright on the bench of the little launch, staring stoically ahead, the three white men noticed his condition. For once he failed to see any humor in a situation that others considered hilarious.

The fair man who knew how to speak had promised Papik that he would feel better on the larger vessel, but he couldn't have been more mistaken. The sealer's speed caused it to pitch and roll in spite of its greater weight, and the sickening smell from the engines did the rest.

Until Papik decided to forget his dignity in front of all the white men, to stretch out on deck and moan mournfully.

Although just a grimy little vessel, the sealer should have seemed an island crammed with novelties to people who considered a five-foot igloo a castle. And in fact Vivi toured it with delighted curiosity, inspecting every cobweb and cockroach, escorted by the captain; who was promptly bitten by Karipari the instant he took the liberty of putting a hand on Vivi's shoulder.

Papik, always flat on his back, eyes shut, was indifferent to the world around him. He didn't care to know how many men were on board, and couldn't have done so had he tried, for he had only twenty between fingers and toes, and the ship carried a handful more than that.

All he wanted was to set foot on the promised floe and never leave it again until it touched land or ice.

Those who required precise figures to retain their bearings have established that some of the floes and bergs that drift southward every summer after breaking off the polar cap or being calved by the glaciers on land, measure over five hundred miles across. However, the floe the sealer was headed for came closer to being the smallest than the largest of the lot. But it had an advantage. It wasn't white but black—with seal. Which so crammed their carrier that they hung over its edge.

And the blackness was speckled with the white coats of the newborn.

Thousands of seal cows had convened on that floe to bear their young and suckle them until they would shed their fluffy baby coats and be old enough to swim. Childbearing time coincides with the breakup of the ice —one more reason why the Men respect the seals' intelligence—and when it comes, the northern seal cows swim southward under the great ice and board the drift-ing pans, turning them into floating maternity wards that will keep their babies safe from the bears.

But only from the bears.

After all had boarded the floe except two crewmen and Vivi, who hid below deck because the seals are ashamed to be seen by a woman while being killed, the ship followed in the wake of the seal patch which was scudding along before a brisk north wind under a cloud-ed sky.

In his sickness Papik hadn't tried to find out how the foreigners would conduct the hunt. On disembarking, the blond man had handed him the same kind of ma-chine-made oak club all the others were holding, and shouted something. Still shaken, Papik remained on the floe's edge.

Roaring like a conquering horde, the club-swinging men lunged into the seal mass, making for the plump white babies.

Having no defense but flight, the mothers retreated, bellowing raucously, and many plunged into the water. The few that dared oppose the attackers with the weight of their bodies were promptly clubbed into submission.

Seeing themselves abandoned to the club-swinging monsters, the babies shrieked in panic. Then men seized them by their hind flippers and bashed in their soft skulls. Then they spun them around, stabbed them in the throat, and stripped away their pelts and the under-lying blubber with swift strokes of their razor-sharp blades. Some little whitecoats escaped their attackers after the first blows and flapped about helplessly on their fins while bleeding from their heads, eyes bulging through the redness. But the maternity ward had be-come a slaughter-house without issue.

As more and more mothers fled into the water and the massacre spread, the ice became one huge field of crimson splashes between pink, skinned carcasses, some still stirring.

Clutching his club, Papik stood gaping. The spectacle had dispelled his sickness. He realized why these men had smeared their ungreased faces with the first blood they had spilled: as a protection against the biting wind. What he couldn't understand was the reason for such wholesale slaughter. To Papik, hunting was life. To the point that he didn't know whether he hunted to live or lived to hunt. But it had always meant food and clothing and implements. This was the first hunt he couldn't enjoy, or understand.

The seals, gentle and generous animals, love the Men, and supply them with all the necessities and most of the joys of life. Small wonder that the Men love the seals, too, and refrain from killing more of them than they need, sparing the rest for future occasions. And sometimes they adopt an orphaned seal pup—the best of all pets, affectionate and playful—and raise it until it is old enough to swim.

Papik couldn't understand either why these hunters' faces had become distorted under their crimson masks —by an expression similar to hate, or lust for blood. Since the Men took pride in the lack of possessions that left them free to roam, Papik was not acquainted with its counterpart, greed.

The sealers worked with furious speed, often neglecting to puncture the throats of their victims. Some babies recovered their senses after being skinned and hobbled around blindly in their pink flesh beaded with blood, until they came to a panting stop, breathing their last, or toppled into the freezing salt water.

Meanwhile many mothers had started coming back, looking for their young. They recognized them also without skin, for the faces remained intact; and they caressed and kissed them, crying pitifully. Some offered their milk to the little carcass, hoping to revive it.

Until they themselves were clubbed to death.

Papik was still standing in a stupor on the floe's edge when a blow in his ribs cut his breath. Two sealers stood at his elbow. One was the blond who knew how to speak.

"Kill!" he snarled with bloodied teeth, shaking his club before Papik's nose. As Papik stared back at him unmoving, the man punched him in the stomach and the other gave him a shove that toppled him.

A tumble on ice is the hardest fall of all; not even a cold-calloused polar skin can shrug it off.

Papik got up at once, seized by the blind frenzy that can overcome even the meekest of Men; and Papik was not the meekest. He gnashed his teeth, his jaw trembled as when sighting the first game after the winter night, then his club went up and cracked down on the blond locks. The white man sagged like a seal pup. Then Papik brained the second one, and went for the others. But this he didn't remember afterward.

He learned it before the trial.

6

He Who Listens

The trial took place at Cape Misery, a promontory of ice-clad land jutting into a deep ocean, where the skipper of the sealing vessel had set Papik ashore, to be dealt with by white men's justice. Under the bird cliffs were a few scattered brown or yellow frame houses roofed with corrugated iron sheets, set up by white men, and some native huts of sod and stones, built to last for the duration of a short summer.

Like the Eskimo dwellings, the rudimentary houses of wood and iron that the white men imported to the desolate regions of the northernmost Arctic usually consisted only of a single room, and a small one at that. But in the settlement at Cape Misery there was a trading post that boasted, in addition, a kitchen, which was the pride of the foreign trader's foreign wife, although the most progressive item it contained was a coal-fed iron stove. And it was in this kitchen that the itinerant judge, Boas, had decided to hold court, for the fire house where some trials had formerly been conducted had burned down.

As Judge Boas was bald and the kitchen drafty, he had donned a coonskin cap complete with tail that he had bought in a toy shop back home, but which he considered better suited to the dignity of his office than the wool skier's cap with which he had arrived from the south.

Most civil servants from the white men's lands who asked to do a stint in the Arctic were either adventurers, idealists, or plain crackpots. Judge Boas was a fishing nut. As to legal-aid counsel Aage, the bright-eyed young man sent to defend Papik, he was an incorrigible idealist.

One sleep earlier, Aage had met the Judge's ship as it dropped anchor in the bay. They had been the guests of Trader Tor, a large brown bear of a man and one of the town's four white residents, but they had refrained from discussing the case in order not to prejudice it. They had drunk just enough spirits to call each other by their first names, but not so much as to wake up hung over and biliously regretting their decision.

In sum, the premises for a fair and pleasant trial were all present.

Judicial procedure is sketchy in the Arctic, and prosecution determinedly lenient and paternalistic with the childish natives.

Nobody was present except Judge Boas who sat at the kitchen table, lawyer Aage, defendant Papik, the white policeman who represented the prosecution, Trader Tor who acted as interpreter, his wife Birgit who had volunteered as Court recorder in order to keep an eye on her kitchen, Vivi out of curiosity, and Karipari, the lead dog, because it had threatened to bite anybody who would separate it from its mistress' side.

After Papik had been charged with homicide and inflicting injuries to two persons in a note read out by the policeman, Aage stated his case:

"One thing we must always bear in mind when judging these people, Boas, Your Honor. Our criminal code

does not always apply in their society, and in recent
years this has been taken increasingly into account. . . ."

Although he found it hard to breathe in the stuffy
kitchen, his big face and bare chest awash in sweat, Papik was proud to be sitting in a privileged position, in
the middle of the room, as the most prominent guest.
Like Vivi, he followed the proceedings with an eager
grin, wondering what was going on.

Lawyer Aage was a newcomer to the legal game, but
he had heard of tragic reactions on the part of Eskimos
who had fallen afoul of white man's justice. Showing
wisdom and shrewdness, he had explained to Papik that
by bashing those human skulls he had also infringed
some of the white men's severest taboos, and that he
would have to make amends.

Papik was the last person on earth to shrug off taboos, and he was grateful to Aage for explaining that he
would probably have to stay confined for some time in a
big house far to the south, close to the tree line, where
Aage would show him exactly how to exorcise the white
man's outraged spirits.

Aage had been so skillful that Papik was looking forward to visiting the southern town while making
amends.

In Eskimo society, crime was mostly confined to murder, and the native way of dealing with it was as simple
as a snow knife. If a murderer was not promptly killed
in revenge by the victim's relatives, he was forever ex-
cluded from the community of Men; a punishment that
often meant death for people whose survival sooner or
later depended on human solidarity.

However, killing under provocation or for reasons of
survival was not considered murder, but merely an accident to be promptly forgotten. Only a malicious killing
was murder—as when a man slew another to appropri-

ate his dogteam or his wife. But such malice was rare among people who were by nature friendly and considerate of their neighbors, to the point of being the only ones on earth who had never known war.

New to the Arctic though he was, Judge Boas was nevertheless aware of all this, having been carefully briefed before being sent north. As a true jurist, he didn't see why local customs should be allowed to cloud the crystalline clarity of the law. However, he knew that any severe sentence would arouse the Greek chorus of the usual protesters back home.

Exposing him to the risk of being recalled before he had gotten in any fishing.

Aage was droning on, largely ignored by the Judge who was trying to reproduce on his pad the superb Dolly Varden trout that Birgit had cooked for her guests. Although he had eaten but a small portion, he had promptly developed the itchy rash above the collarbone that the intake of fish never failed to cause him. In a changing and unpredictable world, this was the one reaction Judge Boas could always rely on.

While he completed his Dolly Varden, interrupting his work from time to time to scratch his collarbone, he wondered whether he would have time to go fishing before moving on to the next case on his agenda, which promised to be specially bothersome for his legal mind —a father accused of slaying and devouring his own daughter. But this also was no crime in Eskimo eyes. Marooned on a floe, the family had been facing starvation. Mother, son, daughter, all had offered their own lives to save the others, until the father had decided to sacrifice the least useful member.

So as not to think about it, Judge Boas reverted his attention to the young attorney.

"They are closer to animals than to human beings,"

Aage was saying. "Eking out the barest living in millions
of square miles of ice and permafrost, often in temperatures colder than 80° Fahrenheit below zero, they have
no written laws, substitute superstition for religion, and
are in fact a weak, depleted, and dying people, locked in
old patterns, unfit to adjust to new ones. So it's our duty
to help them."

"God!" the Judge audibly implored the ceiling. He
prided himself on never losing his cool, and through
sheer strength of character and training, he had taught
himself to shut off his ears as effectively as a seal under
water when he reached a point beyond endurance.

He did so now, picked up his pen again, and started a
new drawing.

The Judge was trying to reproduce that miracle of native inventiveness that was the long harpoon and that he
had seen hanging on the wall of Trader Tor's store. But
it was far too complex a contrivance to remember in de-
tail after a cursory observation or for an amateur artist
to render on paper, and in fact the drawing came out a
disaster. It served nonetheless its intended purpose of
absorbing and thus relaxing him.

"Boas!" Aage called. "Are you with me, Your Hon-
or?"

"I'm listening!" the Judge answered irritably because
he wasn't.

"Thank you, Boas, Your Honor. You see, we have
difficulty just communicating with these people. For one
thing, their language is unrelated to any other in the
world. It lacks many terms we couldn't do without.
Even swear words. To swear, they must borrow ours.
And they have no word for *steal*. Am I right, Tor?"

"Right," said Tor. "They say *take*."

"Nor do they have a word for *guilty* or *innocent*,"
Aage went on.

"Is that so." The Judge sounded unimpressed, and Aage began resenting his attitude.

"Although their language is so complicated that there are more than a thousand forms for the word *man,* depending on the way it is used, it has no word for *God,* much less for *judge!*" he announced vindictively.

"Then who am I?" asked the Judge.

"In translation you come out as He Who Listens."

Judge Boas nodded, bringing his raccoon tail to life. "I like that. He Who Listens. And who are you?"

"I am He Who Talks," Aage said.

"Great! That's the one foreign language I want to learn."

At this point Vivi startled the audience and caused the dog to bark with a rumble in her bearhide trousers, due to the canned vegetables she had been fed—a shock to an exclusively carnivorous stomach. Being a lady, she blushed and hid her face in shame.

But Papik greeted his wife's explosion with such a lusty yell of laughter that even the Judge found it hard to retain a straight face.

"In certain areas," Aage was saying when Judge Boas had finished his latest drawing and shifted his attention back to the proceedings, "we have forbidden the Eskimos to kill more than three seals a year per person, although their whole livelihood depends on seals. This explains why witnessing the slaughter of thousands of seals puzzled and confused my client. Until he was seized by a sudden frenzy—the well-known condition medically called arctic hysteria—and decided to intervene against those who, he believed, were breaking the law. Yes, Boas, Your Honor! It is my contention that my client thought he had to substitute for the absent police and uphold the laws of our great country! How was he to know that we permit our hunters to slaughter no less than 250,000 seals a year? And other governments the slaughter of many more?"

Judge Boas looked at Aage for the first time with real interest. The young man hadn't brought up one valid point yet, but he was beginning to get close.

"In other words," Aage went on, "my client was driven by an irresistible impulse—to establish justice without any rational considerations. And in such cases the law provides unconditional acquittal by reason of temporary insanity."

"So you plead temporary insanity?"

"Yes, Your Honor! But should the Court not feel entitled to set my client free on these grounds, then I propose to consider that he acted in self-defense."

"Self-defense? Please elaborate," the Judge said helpfully.

"When he refused to participate in the slaughter, my client was bodily attacked by the sealers and thought that his life was in danger."

"You're getting warm, Aage," the Judge said. "Go on."

"Thank you, Boas, Your Honor." Delighted by this unexpected encouragement, Aage resumed with renewed enthusiasm:

"Should my thesis of self-defense not be accepted, then I beg the Court to consider my client's action as unintentional manslaughter—inflicting on him a minimal sentence. However," Aage was now fully launched, "should the Court believe that my client's action was intentional, then let it at least concede that at no time was it my client's ultimate design to cause the unfortunate victim's death but, at the most, just to inflict on him the same major concussion, in the way of a lesson, that he inflicted on the other two sealers who seem to be surviving their skull fractures very well. However, if the Court chooses, against all logic, to convict my client of premeditated, intentional murder, then the sentence should be kept very light, since for these people a permanence in jail equals a death warrant—and we have abolished the death sentence long ago."

"Huh? I don't follow."

"It's an established fact, Your Honor, that no true Eskimo has as yet survived for any length of time in one of our towns—and much less so in the confines of a jail."

"But that's no legal point, Aage, my friend," the Judge said in a tone of paternal reproach.

"Still, we must take it into consideration."

"Now carry on, Aage, and wind it up, for God's sake."

"Certainly, Boas. To conclude, my client throws himself on the mercy of the Court, and the Court should appreciate that by waiving a jury trial my client saves our taxpayers a considerable amount of money. Just assembling the necessary witnesses generally proves very expensive and often impossible in these parts."

"How come?"

"Most of the time they are all scattered at sea or busy sealing on some other floe."

Judge Boas looked up sharply. "Some *other* floe, you said? This thing didn't happen on a floe, did it?"

"Yes, of course, Boas. On a floe. On drifting ice."

"You never said it, Aage, my friend," the Judge said softly. "I assumed you knew it. It must be in the police record."

Flustered, the Judge riffled through his papers. "Here's merely the sworn report of the ship's captain as taken down by the police. I assumed the homicide occurred on his ship."

"It occurred in the course of a big seal hunt, Boas," Aage said with pointed deliberation. "And seal herds usually convene in the sea or on the ice or on beaches, but never—I repeat, *never*—on board ships."

The Judge was piqued. "Show me the precise location where it occurred," he snapped.

"Approximately here," the policeman said, dusting the map.

"The Court doesn't want approximation!" The Judge found it suddenly very hard to retain his cool.

"But, Boas," Aage said, "it's impossible to pinpoint the precise location for a floe."

The policeman put in: "It was adrift hundreds of miles from land at the time."

The Judge flicked his pen down on the table, leaned back, and drew a deep breath. Then, looking at Aage, he said:

"You're wasting the Court's time, my good man."

"I don't understand."

"Of course, you don't! This thing happened hundreds of miles from any shore, right? Not on a ship, not on an airplane, but on a floe, sailing under no flag, pertaining to no nation, drifting in extraterritorial waters. Extraterritorial! Do you get the legal implications? No Court in the world has jurisdiction over what is done in extraterritorial waters, by a man without nationality, born somewhere on the arctic ice. So he can't be brought to trial! And I'm throwing this case out of Court."

"But . . . but. . . ." Aage stammered.

"I have no choice! And because your client obviously needs legal help from on high, the Court now orders his immediate release."

Aage had flushed, while the bystanders looked perplexed. Even Papik and Vivi sensed that not all was right.

"I appeal, Your Honor!" Aage shrieked, his voice breaking.

The Judge inquired icily: "And why, pray, should you appeal, when the Court sets your client free?"

"I . . . I appeal the motivation!" Aage sputtered. "It's offensive to my professional standing!"

"You haven't any standing left, my good man!"

"Let me remind you that I didn't bring the charges! The State did!"

"And let me remind you that charges are brought automatically when a homicide takes place. The session is over." The Judge rose, gathering his papers.

Aage moved toward the table, breathing deep. "If you are so smart, why didn't you first study the case as your duty requires?"

The Judge turned purple, his self-control snapping all at once, and roared: "Shut up! I said the session is over!"

"Now, Boas! Accusing *me,* in order to hide your own inadequacy!"

"Inadequacy?! I'll have you disbarred if you don't apologize this instant! You're sick! Sick! And don't you dare call me Boas again! I'm still the Judge to you"

"Not when the session is over!"

Papik plucked his attorney's sleeve, but Aage elbowed him away and went on loudly trading opinions with the Judge. Papik then got hold of Tor's sleeve and asked:

"How about a man's stay in town?"

"No stay in town," Tor said.

"No stay in town?" Papik echoed indignantly.

"The white man had promised!" Vivi protested.

"No stay in town," Tor confirmed.

Papik had been patient, which had cost him considerable effort, and courteous, which came naturally to him. But too much was too much. The two foreigners stood shouting at each other over the table, ignoring their guests. Papik didn't like to do it, but somebody had to teach them manners, for their own good.

So he seized He Who Speaks by the collar of his nylon parka and He Who Listens by the collar of his windbreaker and banged their heads together.

"Get this animal out of my hair!" shrieked the Judge, forgetting that he was bald.

Everybody had risen, shouting for calm or contributing otherwise to the confusion—including Karipari. Up to that point, the dog's behavior had been exemplary. But on seeing its master grappling with the two strangers, the husky pounced on them and succeeded in drawing blood from both, for all its flattened fangs. It wasn't Karipari's fault that the white men had buttery buttocks and didn't wear dogproof pants.

At that juncture the policeman remembered his peacemaking role and discharged his pistol toward the ceiling, and Papik, startled, let go of his quarries.

The moans of the two bitten men established order and silence in the courtroom, except for Karipari's persisting growls and Vivi's shouts ordering her dog to keep quiet.

The injuries were not serious but painful, especially for the Judge, as they ruled out any fishing on his part for weeks to come, and he salved his wounded feelings by sentencing Papik on the spot to ten months for assault and battery, besides contempt of Court, assigning him to the custody of his attorney.

Not wanting to let Aage go scot-free either.

7

Taboos

If Papik knew anything, he knew this: while the Powers that rule the Men are awesome, those that rule white men are even worse.

And taboos were made to be obeyed, not understood.

His experience with white men went back to his adolescence, to the time when he had lost his parents. They had both died from natural causes: his father bled white from a wound suffered in killing two bears; his mother by drowning, a suicide, as she wished to rejoin her husband in Paradise, and not be a burden to anyone.

Thereafter Papik had escorted, together with a few other Men, an expedition of explorers. On that occasion he learned that the best thing to do in the company of foreigners was not to do anything. It was the only way a Man could hope not to violate any of their taboos.

One incident above all had shown him the power of their spirits.

The white men had a strict taboo against eating rotted meat—which might be the reason, Papik surmised, why they were so grumpy. During the trek, the explorers had tasted, and even got to like, the native foods, avoiding only the rotted meats. Until the bravest among them resolved to defy his own spirits and break the old taboo.

He grimaced on savoring the first morsel of seal rendered tender and fragrant by the process of decay, but he went on munching intrepidly until he had consumed a sizable portion.

It actually killed him.

What most impressed Papik was the swiftness with which the foreign spirits struck. The transgressor was still picking his teeth when all at once he turned green in the face and pressed both hands to his stomach. But the outraged spirits didn't let him go that easily. They made him writhe in pain for two turns of the sun, while his alarmed companions performed various exorcisms like pouring magic liquids down the sinner's throat and forcing mysterious solids up his rear.

All for naught.

Of course, the Men ran away from the dead explorer, terrified of his ghost; not so his companions. They weren't even afraid of touching the corpse with their bare hands—for a Man, the ultimate folly. And yet not one of them died from it, whereas their companion had died merely from eating a forbidden delicacy.

One thing was established once and for all in Papik's mind after that: foreigners have different taboos, and a wise Man had better abide by them while in their company.

Not only was Papik grateful to Aage for undertaking to show him how to appease such baleful spirits, but Aage also was vaguely grateful to Papik for enabling him to satisfy his desire to help his neighbor.

By the Judge's decision, Papik was even closer to him than any neighbor: assigned to Aage's custody, he was, at first, his tenant and guest.

Aage had taken his ward by ship to the southern town where he was stationed. He wanted to take Vivi along also, for Papik's comfort; but the dogs were not invited, and if they couldn't go, Vivi couldn't go, his team being a Man's only riches. So Vivi remained at Cape Misery with Tor and his wife Birgit, to help in their trading post.

Located at the mouth of a fjord, below the dog frontier but still well above the tree line, the town was in the deep South and very populous by Papik's standards, far up North and very small by Aage's—numbering a couple of thousand souls and existing mostly by and for the white men's fishing industry, for which Papik was going to work as a means of exorcism.

Although inhabited mainly by Eskimos, the town was the administrative seat in the Arctic of the Supreme Police, as the natives called the white men's government. It lay on a rough territory of granite rocks interspersed with moss and lichen and puddles of half-frozen mud, not yet snow-clad when Aage and Papik reached it in late fall. The frame houses, raised on blocks of cement and scattered about in wild disarray as if dropped from the sky, had been prefabricated in white man's country and sent by ship to that woodless region; mostly small cabins with peaked roofs and a few rambling apartment buildings.

The single street, starting at the harbor and cutting the town in half, led nowhere, but it was flanked by a few isolated shops filled with white men's wares. To reach the dwellings behind them, one had to tramp over the assorted refuse that the occupants threw out of the windows and through the mud that caked one's boots.

That was the South.

Papik marveled at the bands of unattended children he saw everywhere, busy smoking or begging tobacco from passers-by, and at the total absence of roaming dogs. Aage explained that since the town lay just below the Arctic Circle, which roughly corresponded to the dog frontier, where the Eskimos' economy did not depend on sleds, the police had orders to shoot on sight any unleashed dog, to insure the children's safety.

Papik asked what was the purpose of keeping so many children alive, but for once Aage was unable to give a good answer to a good question.

Aage lodged his ward in his own home—a small flat entirely furnished in the white men's way, in a large building that housed only members of the Supreme Police—and treated him like an honored guest. So did Aage's wife, a petite and pretty blonde. She gamely overlooked the disheveled appearance of Papik, who hadn't been rasped clean by Vivi since sunup, and the state of his hides, which hadn't been washed with urine for just as long.

However, with the very first meal the problem of food came up. To be polite, Papik gulped everything that was offered him, but his hosts could see that he wasn't happy; and Aage, complementing the few words in his repertory with sign language, promised him more suitable viands in the future. The seal herds that formerly abounded in these waters had been exterminated by the white men, but now and then a long-distance swimmer from the northern waters strayed into some trawler's net and showed up at the fishmarket. And then there was always caribou to be had, frozen or smoked or dried.

But Papik wasn't hungry. His stomach was still upset by the rough, interminable sea voyage, having to sit on a chair put his massive thighs to a severe test, and moreover he felt near stifling in the closed, heated quarters. Sweat trickled from his bare chest into his birdskin trousers and dripped audibly on the elegant linoleum floor.

When, after dinner, Aage indicated that he wanted him to retire to another room, Papik got up and faced the lady of the house with a conqueror's stance and a winsome grin. He hoped that a bit of laughter with that exotic little woman might brighten these dark times. Since Aage didn't pronounce the expected invitation, Papik addressed him a questioning glance, then stepped closer to the hostess, snickering into her face.

The young woman appeared startled. Then she wrinkled her nose, as her likes did upon catching a bad smell, and looked to her husband for help.

Since wrinkling one's nose meant No among the Men, Papik's interpretation was not far amiss, and his grin waned. So these people had no heart for one who was alway from his wife. So they callously ignored the most elementary rules of hospitality. So what. Papik had one more evidence that all foreigners were peevish churls who had nothing else in mind but to belittle and offend the Men. And why? Because—there could be no other explanation—they envied them.

Papik was too well-bred and superior a man to manifest his disapproval except by pouting.

The next day he started working in the cod factory, an imposing building of glass and concrete erected along the pierside by a white men's enterprise.

Regardless of how low the temperatures dropped during the arctic night, a warm sea current kept the fjord navigable the year round, and trawlers from different nations, smashing their way through the floating ice, could come up even in the dead of winter and unload their hauls of cod directly into the factory, to be dried, salted, or frozen before being shipped south.

The factory employed far more men and women than Papik could count. The manager and some overseers were white men, but the labor force was made up of southern Eskimos. As the Eskimos had a way of disappearing after payday or going fishing whenever they felt like it, the manager was glad to take on a trusty who couldn't leave his job before he had served his sentence.

The only condition was that Papik should first go under a shower and scrub himself with brush and soap. Overawed by the surroundings, Papik submitted meekly to this new indignity, as part of the punishment. Then he was made to don the worker's unform—wooden clogs designed to keep his feet dry, wool socks to keep them warm, and the first woven trousers and shirt of his life, topped by white overalls and a round cap into which he had to tuck his long black hair. The white men's endless taboos included one against getting greasy hairs into cleaned fish.

He was assigned to a machine that took up an entire hall and was so noisy that it prevented any conversation. The contraption started close to the ceiling, with a metal slide serviced by two men standing on an iron platform.

One of the two was Papik.

A moving staircase carried up to them a steady stream of codfish, which had to be sent gliding headfirst down the slide, one at a time. From his vantage point, Papik could see how mechanical blades chopped the heads and tails off the fish just before they were swallowed up by the machine, which then spewed out skinned fillets onto a conveyor belt to the left and the wastage onto a similar belt to the right. Along each belt a line of workers, all dressed in the same funny way as Papik, put the fillets or the waste into handcarts that others wheeled out of the hall when they were full. And that was all.

Nothing else ever happened.

After the novelty had palled, the monotony of the proceedings began afflicting Papik with unbearable boredom, and he started taking bites out of the fish before sending them down the slide; not because he was in need of food, but because the only affliction he had known until then had been hunger, and eating the only cure. This time the expected result did not set in. Soon he felt glutted with cod, but not a bit happier.

Abruptly, machines and noises stopped, and Papik's companion told him that it was time to eat.

The workers filed into a room furnished with long tables and straight chairs all made of real wood, the most valuable material Papik knew, and of which he admired the perfect symmetry. He admired less the food: potatoes and fishballs disguised by a thick sauce. He was glad he had eaten his fill on the platform.

Everybody ate with the same dangerous weapons of shining metal that Papik had seen in use at Aage's table and that he had prudently left alone, not wanting to injure his mouth or risk an eye.

Observing his fellow workers as they ate, Papik discovered that many of them were crossbreeds, of a lighter coloring than real Men, with features that clearly betrayed the admixture of watered blood. He saw no teeth worn down from chewing skins, but all the teeth looked shaky or rotten and were the color of tabacco. Small wonder. Men and women smoked fiercely, and the pipe smokers even used up the others' butts, then tilted the hot ashes into their mouth and munched them with relish. All spoke a bastard Eskimo, which was hard to understand, and they resorted to foreign words for foreign objects instead of circumscribing them. So they used the white men's term to designate the mess hall instead of calling it the Place Where People Eat, as a real Man would have done.

It didn't matter much, for they spoke rarely, and laughed less. Papik had never known so many people to laugh so little.

When the bell rang again, everybody resumed work, without any change at all, until another ringing bell put an end to the ordeal. Dazed and tired, Papik staggered toward the exit and the friendly face of Aage, who had come to take him home and tell him that the overseer was very satisfied with him.

Papik tittered scornfully at this announcement. So the ability of dropping dead fish headfirst down a slide was sufficient to earn praise in this town.

However, not all was well with him.

Ever since the time his mother had licked him clean after dropping him into the ice hole over which she had been kneeling, Papik's body hadn't been touched by water, and the only detergents it had experienced were blubber, urine, or saliva. So the scrubbing with hot water and soap in the factory shower caused his skin to break into a rash just as he laid himself down to sleep and that kept him awake with a maddening itch.

Which he endured stoically, assuming it was part of the spirits' retaliation.

Because he had kept the window open all night, the next morning the radiator in his room burst, flooding the building and causing considerable damage; whereupon Aage arranged to let him bunk in the factory's cooling room.

Papik wasn't much happier there. The temperature was endurable, but he missed the open air and physical exertion; or a good winter sleep. Every time, before he could drift into a proper torpor, the bell would rout him out of his slumber and summon him back to work, whereupon he could never get properly awake. By then, the murky daylight lasted only an hour or two, but the townspeople worked and slept just as long in winter as in summer, deliberately ignoring the rhythm of nature.

Together with his gaiety and joy of life, Papik's appetite also was fading—a worrisome symptom. This was the season when a Man's girth should about equal his height; but during the long wait for the judge to arrive at

Cape Misery, and then for the boat headed south, and the voyage interrupted by calls at coastal villages, he had put on little flesh that summer, and now he felt listless and miserable. He who used to enjoy human company began to shun it, preferring to mope in solitude.

Here nobody knew or cared that he was a great hunter. He resented the general indifference, if not downright contempt. Of course no one held it against him that he had killed a white man; it had been clearly an accident, due to a fit of rage, for which only the victim was responsible. But some couldn't forgive him for looking different. More than one had the gall to smile amusedly over his head of hair that he wore uncut and unkempt, in a manly way; whereas these southern Eskimos tried to resemble the effete foreigners in all things, even making it a point of never eating raw meat or fish, except on the sly. And those who didn't go hunting and fishing on Sundays went to church instead, conspicuously clutching their Holy Book, even if they couldn't read, and keeping their amulets carefully hidden, lest the preacher should fly into a rage.

Thus Papik made the startling discovery that many southern Eskimos admired the foreigners, and pretended not to know that their polar brothers, and they alone, represented the aristocracy of Men.

Well, Papik wasn't here for fun, nor to be revered, but to expiate; and this he was doing.

He was allowed to stroll about town after work, watching the bands of children at their stupid games. It wasn't really their fault if they had nothing serious to do. Their greatest thrill, besides cadging tobacco from strangers and picking up butts, was to smash windowpanes with rocks without getting caught.

The town was lit with electricity, and the round-the-clock whir of the electric works converting fuel into kil-

owatts and smelling up the air was the dominant noise
—muffled by the snow that had started falling abun-
dantly, blanketing the puddles of frozen mud and lichens with a uniform whiteness.

The shop windows exhibited every kind of white
men's wares and mechanical gadgets. The more mysterious they looked, the less they interested Papik. He could
appreciate a hunting knife of shining steel, but he dis-
missed more complicated objects as white men's witchcraft, with which he wanted no truck. But the first time
he spotted a caribou hide and quarters of its carcass
nailed against a house wall to dry, he tarried before it at
length, his heart filling with unbearable yearning for the
thrill of the hunt.

During mealtimes, a fellow worker named Pilutok
succeeded at last in cracking the ice of Papik's resentment with the warmth of his smiles and the revelation
that he himself hailed from above the dog frontier. He
had come to the conclusion that town life was the best
after he had lost his wife and partner and their collective
son and team in an icebreak, and the police had trans-
ported him, badly broken, by sled and ship to the hospital in this town.

Pilutok didn't use the foreign word for hospital, but
an Eskimo definition: the Place Where People Undress;
further inspiring Papik to confide in him.

"The Men here are not friendlier than foreigners," he
complained. "One can't walk into a house and help himself to food if not invited."

"There is a reason," Pilutok said, and spat into his
plate. "Everybody owes money to the stores. If the debts
grow too big, the stores stop giving. And one also needs
money to buy beer in the Place of Loud Music. And
that," Pilutok smirked, "is where a man finds his
laughs."

"Married women?"

Pilutok wrinkled his nose. "Single. You need nobody's permission but the woman's."

Women were always an interesting subject, and their table companions also started following the conversation.

"Don't the men take wives of their own?" Papik asked.

"Not if they can help it. Here you buy your clothes at the store. You don't need a woman to sew for you. And the women don't depend on men for food because they also buy everything in stores, from their wages. If they don't work, the Supreme Police gives them wages for doing nothing."

"Don't the men want sons?"

"Sons?" Pilutok spat in his plate again, as it was forbidden to spit on the floor. "What for? The Supreme Police takes care of a man until he dies. You've seen the oldsters sitting on the benches, with nothing to do but wait for death."

"But what does a woman do with her children?"

"She can bring them to the Place for Orphans."

"How does one ask for a woman, if there is no husband to talk to?"

"You don't," Pilutok said. "She asks you. The women outnumber us because they last longer than we if nobody kills them. And even the very old ones have only one thing on their minds."

"What do you want with very old women?"

Pilutok tittered. "Haven't you found out yet? Even if she can't soften boots, a toothless woman can satisfy a man in small ways better than young women with long teeth!"

For once their table companions also laughed loudly.

"You had the good sense to leave your wife behind," Pilutok concluded, slapping Papik's thigh. "Somebody will show you how to get your laughs."

8

The Town

The Place of Loud Music where Pilutok took Papik on payday was sweltering with people, cloudy with smoke, redolent with beer, and so resonant that Papik's eardrums ached, hardened though they were to the noise of the cod factory.

As a prisoner, he couldn't go without a surveillant, and Aage, forever helpful, had consented to accompany him. He wouldn't let Papik drink beer, but he allowed him to smoke. And Papik was glad that Aage knew so well what was permitted and what was taboo.

Papik had winced at the taste of beer once or twice before, in his fleeting contacts with white men. His experience with tobacco had been only a trifle less terrible. But this time, though it made him cough, he puffed away determinedly at anything that was offered him; first because he saw that everybody smoked, and then because he assumed that since it was one of the few things permitted, the white spirits looked upon tobacco smoking with favor.

So he watched the proceedings with eyes that watered from the smoke but were wide with amazement.

There was no dearth of women, all of them native and many of them old. And there were also a few foreigners. Most of the white men in that frontier town were either staid civil servants like Aage or hirsute hellions employed by the fishing industry or the building contractors—usually the roughest and toughest of their tribes, come north without wives of their own for a stint of hard work at high wages.

The tables were crowded with bottles and the dance floor with men in shirtsleeves and women in town dresses who all exerted themselves with great energy to a savage beat wafted by a brightly lit box. Although only beer was available, everybody was in high spirits and many appeared drunk, wavering on wobbly legs, faces dripping from the effort and the heat. Papik recognized several men and women from the cod factory; usually taciturn on the job, they now were as excited as the rest.

Pilutok, Papik's companion, was one of the most active. He whirled around the floor like a snowflake or weaved among the tables in search of ever new partners; with scant success, despite his enthusiasm and previous boasting. Although his name meant Little Leaf, he was a short-set, smelly, sweating blubber-barrel, who kept being spurned by the ladies he invited to dance or abandoned by the few who chanced it. After each failure, he would dash to the counter for another bottle of beer and then flit off, with renewed energies, to a new venture.

Pilutok was not the only one who kept changing partners. Most couples did, although they hugged each other tightly while they danced, keeping their eyes closed and pawing one another. Many women were more forward than the men; especially the riper ones. Papik was scandalized by the behavior of one so old that she should have wandered off into the night to die if she had had any decency; but she was trying to hug young men instead, and drag them to the dance floor to kiss them in the indecent way of the white men. Not for her the tender nose rubbing and snuffing at the other's face.

"This happens in all your towns?" Papik asked Aage, who was watching with visible disapproval.

"Not quite. Here the women drink faster, speak louder, and bear more children—especially the unmarried ones."

"Why?"

Although he had made considerable progress in learning the language, Aage didn't know how to say all that was on his mind. He tried anyway.

"You people are by nature much friendlier than others. Alcohol makes your women too friendly, and sometimes your men too forward. We know the dangers of alcohol. You don't. Do you understand?"

"No." And Papik returned his attention to the frolicking crowd.

The white men danced with the prettiest and the youngest girls, who seemed to prefer them to their own people. And their behavior was clearly a prelude to more intimate laughter. Just as Papik was beginning to wonder about that, Pilutok volunteered the explanation, during one of his brief stops at the table:

"The women in this town believe that bearing a white man's child brings good luck."

However, there were still some Eskimo women who appreciated real Men and knew one when they smelled him. At least one woman did—a lady in a screaming red dress who wasn't the youngest of the lot but still had all her teeth, and whose tawny complexion and blue-black hair assigned her to a tribe as yet unwatered by white blood. Plainly smitten by Papik's matted mane and wind-whipped visage, she signaled and smiled at him while dancing with others. When she resolutely seized his hand and tried to yank him off his chair while he clung to the table for dear life, even Aage threw back his head and laughed.

It was to Papik's own immense surprise that he re-fused to follow the lady's solicitation, for he had always dreamed the impossible dream of finding droves of fe-males without effort. But now he discovered that he didn't like those outlandish ways anymore than getting codfish conveyed to him by an endless escalator.

When the good lady came back for a second try, Pilu-tok sighted her and grabbed hold of her. While bobbing and bumping around the floor with this new partner, he loudly informed her that Papik was his brother and was staying with him.

Good-natured as ever, Papik did not deny it.

The evening's final surprise came when, unable to de-cide whether his hands should serve him to rub his smarting eyes or stop his aching ears, Papik decided to leave and discovered that his bearhide parka had disap-peared.

He vowed to kill the taker the instant he set eyes on him, but Aage said it was a job for the police; and Papik was surprised to hear that the role of the police wasn't confined to shooting dogs and arresting Men. As Aage pointed out, no one wore bearhides in this town, but mostly windbreakers of cloth lined with make-believe fur, from the stores, and if Aage used his official power and unleashed the entire four-men police force, there was a good chance to recover Papik's parka.

Aage proved right.

Papik needed a little time to learn the new ways and to discover that women who belong to nobody belong to everybody. After a couple of sleeps disturbed by thoughts, he resolved to return to the Place of Loud Music with a more open mind. But the evil spirits inter-fered once more with his highflying designs.

He had been feeling wretched for several days. No doubt, the spirits were working on him; but since he was following all of Aage's instructions designed to appease them, he waited confidently for his wretchedness to pass. Instead, it kept worsening—the knot in his stomach, the spike in his head, the ache under his ears. He felt hot and then cold. He sweated and shivered. And when he started seeing two codfish in his hand when he had picked up but one, he knew he had had it.

And finally he passed out on the job.

He woke up in a hospital ward, after his companion on the platform had managed to get hold of him just as he was about to topple into the slide, risking the loss of his head, tail, and skin in the machine.

He felt dizzy and nauseated. He was clad in a white shirt and was lying on a cot, one of two long rows. Through the open door, he could see another, similar ward. He had never suspected that there were that many sick people in the world. This was the northernmost hospital built by the white men to take care of sick and wounded people within a territory stretching upward for thousands of miles.

A young white man and two Eskimo women, all dressed in white smocks and wafting sickening smells, were moving from cot to cot, examining the patients. The older nurse bared Papik's chest and asked him how he felt.

"Not good," Papik mumbled.

"He feels close to dying," the nurse translated.

"Something seems terribly wrong," exclaimed the doctor, staring at the fist-sized bulge pumping spasmodically on his patient's chest.

"It's only a greatly enlarged heart," the nurse said. "You'll see it in most of our men from the North."

The doctor went to work on Papik in the way of the white angakoks, feeling his pulse, pinching and knocking and squeezing him. When his ears were pressed, the patient let out a howl, and the doctor laughed—the strangest exorcism Papik had ever witnessed.

"You have a children's disease," the nurse informed him, tittering.

Although coming down with the mumps as an adult was no laughing matter, yet it was always funny to discover that a big brute of a man had caught a child's ailment. But Papik couldn't join in the laughter, for it hurt his ears when he tried.

The younger nurse then stuck a needle in his buttock, but Papik wasn't the type to take a jab with a needle lying down, especially from a woman. He bounced from his cot with a growl, but before he could get at the nurse's throat the doctor circled him from behind and shouted for help from the other patients. In spite of his condition, Papik put up a good fight, but was finally subdued and given another, different injection. One that put him out for a good stretch.

Papik's malady was long and painful. Every time some harmless southern infection had come to Eskimos who had been free from contagion for countless generations, the uninured bodies proved so helpless that those who succumbed outnumbered those who recovered.

Papik, as usual, belonged to the minority. But his convalescence was slow and dreary, allowing him a lot of time for thought.

Their pitiless surroundings had long weeded out not only the fragile but also the dull-witted among the Men, developing a fairly intelligent strain; and that he himself was one of the most intelligent of the strain, Papik had never seen fit to doubt. Hence he realized that so long as the white men wanted him to stay down south with them he couldn't get away. Here they were stronger than he, mainly because they were allied with devilish spirits that enabled them, among other things, to inject black magic into an honest man's flesh, putting him to sleep. On the other hand he knew from experience that on the ice he would again be safe from them, as the great cold numbed the foreign spirits and rendered them harmless.

For comfort he thought back to the time when his father, Ernenek, had been arrested for accidentally killing a white explorer who had insulted him by spurning his hospitality. Two foolish policemen had sledged all over the northern ice for a couple of years before locating him, and while he was being taken south in shackles, his guardian angel had split open the ocean, engulfing the police sled. Most of the dogs drowned, and one of the policemen died after he had been fished out because his drenched clothes froze instantly in the ripping gale, encasing him in ice and stopping his heart. Since all the provisions and weapons also were lost, the other policeman was at Ernenek's mercy. But instead of abandoning him to the fate he deserved, Ernenek chose to humiliate him by saving his life. Eventually, the policeman proved grateful, reporting that Ernenek had died and could be scratched from the Wanted list.

All this proved that if the Men were helpless and ignorant in the South, the foreigners were just as ignorant and helpless in the North—and Papik should return there to stay as soon as he could.

His weakness persisted long after the pain and swelling were gone, and he felt like drifting into a long restoring winter sleep despite the heat, if the doctor and nurses hadn't kept waking him up to handle and feed him.

Friend Aage also came to cheer him up, usually with slabs of raw caribou. Once he presented him with a hunk of seal meat. But the sight of the thick-grained redness marbled with fat only made Papik miserable with nostalgia without satisfying his palate, which preferred live seal or rotted or frozen.

And once Aage brought news from home.

He had received from Trader Tor a letter that had taken half the winter to reach town on its wayward course by sled and ship. Tor wrote that Vivi was well and awaiting Papik's return.

"Naturally she is waiting," Papik said. "She knows that if she leaves with another man, both will be killed."

Aage winced. "No, no! When will you learn that you can't go around killing people? You were lucky once, but next time they will lock you up and keep you in."

"Who will? A man will be safe on the ice."

"The police will look for you until they find you."

For an instant Papik's large face brightened.

"The police! They would return a man's wife, just as they found his parka."

"It's not the same. They can't bring you back Vivi."

"You mean the police would allow a man to take another's wife?"

"A woman can do what she wants, Papik—according to our laws."

"Not according to ours. A man can't allow his wife to be taken away, and retain his honor."

"You must learn to live with our laws."

Papik knew it was not polite to contradict foreigners, for they just didn't know better, and he did so only with the greatest reluctance.

"We don't go to your land bringing our laws," he said patiently. "Why do you come to our land bringing yours?"

"We consider it our land," Aage said. "I am sorry to say this, but it is, since we are stronger."

Papik stifled a quick laugh, and Aage sighed.

"I'm only trying to help you, Papik. Probably I can

convince the Supreme Police to let you go sooner, as you are not well. So be patient a little longer. And I am sure that you will find Vivi waiting for you."

Papik grinned. "That's what a stupid man told you."

9

Siorakidsok

The Supreme Police let Papik go before the time, but it was a long, slow journey back to Cape Misery, and it was autumn and the sea frozen again when he rejoined Vivi.

She welcomed him with a smile that was tempered with much restraint. The restraint was for the bystanders' benefit, not for Papik's, who didn't even look at her, lest anybody suspect him of having missed her. So he didn't notice that she had put on considerable flesh around the waist during his absence.

She pointed it out to him when they retired to her little room to discuss affairs of mutual interest.

Vivi had some news that was good and some that was bad. The good: although Papik had been away for almost a year, she was pregnant. The bad: all the signs and portents that indicate the coming baby's sex had been alarmingly vague and contradictory, and something had to be done about it fast.

Papik hadn't listened to Vivi's second announcement. He was mulling over the first.

"Have you looked at the full moon in my absence?"

"All the time," Vivi said quickly.

However, a man of the world like Papik was aware that not only the light of the full moon could render a woman pregnant, and he asked: "Have you by any chance also laughed with some man?"

Vivi blushed up to her eyeballs. "It is not impossible."

Papik took a deep breath. "A man must be getting absent-minded. He can't remember having been asked or given permission."

Vivi faced him squarely. "You are right, as usual." She forced her beautiful lips to smile. "But there was no way to ask you and no time to waste. You were impatient for a son. Can you remember that?"

"Yes," Papik conceded miserably.

The stray dogs at Cape Misery had banded together in packs of ten or twelve, each ruled by one that was capable of subduing the others. One such natural leader was Karipari. Engaged in housework and unable to feed all her dogs, Vivi had not been able to keep the pack together, and they had scattered. Karipari's followers included some dogs of Papik's original team and some new ones, and Papik took over the whole pack for the sled on arrival. Karipari had not been admitted into any household, for he kept biting whoever dared so much as approach Vivi.

So Papik and Vivi left town (town? four white men and some forty Eskimos when all the men were home, which was never) in the autumn twilight, on a sled built of bones and anything frozen, glad to resume their trip to the angakok after the long interruption.

The parting from Tor and Birgit was celebrated with many compliments and promises. White men don't share the Eskimos' view that departures are sad and should be ignored. They seem to enjoy farewells, as if they were happy to part company.

"They are nice but stupid," Vivi told Papik as soon as the sled pulled out.

"Not stupid, just ignorant," Papik said. "Like all foreigners."

"How true! Until a silly woman told them, they had no idea that the northeastern wind is male and is called Nakrahyak. That the northwestern is his wife, Pettahrak. And the southeastern is Kahdannek, their daughter."

"A man is not surprised," Papik laughed, cracking the whip over his team. "Many white men don't even know that He Who Walks is the bear, anymore than He Who Runs is the dog."

Vivi laughed so hard at this that she lost her hold on the upright and was almost thrown from the sled, which was skidding and dancing more than usual, for the team was not yet broken in.

"But remember this," Papik said. "Even the nicest foreigners can be dangerous because they are as crazy as wolverines. Nothing about them makes sense—police, laws, spirits. And the only way to be safe is to keep away from them."

But first they had to reach the village at the cove that had been Vivi's home for a long time. According to information not older than two or three years, Siorakidsok was still living there.

If the oldest of all angakoks couldn't help Vivi bear a male son, nobody could.

The sun had spiraled itself out of the sky, allowing the sea to harden, but daylight was still on—the best period for traveling—and they were making good headway, skating over the white expanses under which the ocean rumbled, skirting wind-carved icebergs imprisoned in the seacrust, and strips of dark, naked land ribbed with glaciers.

The Polar Men's regular circuit encompasses the hoary heads of three continents—America, Asia, and Europe—and territories that several nations call their own, provided they can find the borders. And they can, every time.

But only on their maps.

The Men journey to Beartongue Channel for driftwood, to White Wall for birdskins, to Funny Bay for walrus ivory, to Ghostly Gulch for soapstone, to Laughing Inlet for caribou, to Brown Plains for musk ox. On the perennial ice, only a scattering of seals and some wandering bear are to be found.

When there are no angakoks to seek out, no interference from the police, no icebreaks or icequakes, no loss of dogs or mischief from the spirits, no murder or mayhem, a sled may require two years to come full circle. If it takes longer, nobody complains. The Men are in no hurry, being convinced that speed does not lengthen life, but shortens it.

For once, however, Papik and Vivi were impatient to get some place. A new life was noticeably growing in Vivi's innards, and they could take no chances with its sex. They had to reach omniscient Siorakidsok before delivery.

They did.

The Men didn't count the years and never knew how old they were—except Siorakidsok. When they had last seen him, he used to say that he was three hundred years old—fifteen men counted to the end. Now, a handful of years later, he claimed to be four hundred. Some people suspected him of exaggerating, but Siorakidsok peevishly contended that angakoks didn't reckon like common mortals.

He was not only one of the oldest and deafest Men alive but also one of the liveliest—though just a wizened little runt, lost in mangy doghides, paralyzed from the waist down, with no teeth left in his big mouth and little hair on his big head, which was all ears, nose, and lips. His legs had so shrunk through disuse that he seemed to be squatting on his trunk. His detractors asserted that his palsy had been caused by idleness, at a time when he was so powerful that he could always find enough back-scratchers willing to carry him on his caribou rug.

But then the arrival of a missionary at the cove had caused his downfall.

The bearded, awesome-looking white man had come to preach poverty to the poor while leading what was to them a life of luxury, and the community of goods that they had always practiced, while he himself forbade touching the mission stores. He had also persuaded the villagers that believing in the effectiveness of amulets— which he ripped from their necks with his bare hands— and in angakoks was a sin that would lead them into an eternal fire. And the Eskimos didn't dare ignore the warnings of someone who belonged to the most baleful race in the world. But neither did they dare renounce their various amulets, which from then on they kept carefully hidden under their clothes.

Then the missionary had refused to unite in a Christian ceremony Papik with Vivi, and Papik's sister, Ivaloo, with Milak, because the young men were heathens who couldn't be married to the recently baptized girls unless they settled in the village and took lessons in Christianity for a year or two. So the two couples had eloped. Eventually, the missionary also departed, leaving his flock thoroughly bewildered, with a whole new set of frightening taboos to cope with, and wondering how their forefathers had ever managed to survive without the guidance of white missionaries.

They tried playing it safe and to incur neither the foreign nor their own spirits' wrath.

Meanwhile nobody dared put the angakok out on the ice, where a man his age belonged. The villagers were afraid of what his ghost might do to them. And those who remembered the missionary's warnings feared in addition the punishment of the white men's Top Spirit who forbade all killings—even of oldsters and infants.

But ever more people stopped pampering and kowtowing to Siorakidsok. A few villagers merely dropped some ptarmigan stomachs or other discards at his door, to keep him breathing and on the chance that his spook might remember their generosity after death and not come around frightening them in the dark. Siorakidsok had to drag himself out of his hovel of sod and stones on his hands to get at his dole. So all in all the old man had had a hard time of it.

Until Papik and Vivi looked in on him.

Beyond the old caribou skin on which he crouched and his dog garments worn to the hide, there was nothing Siorakidsok could call his own except his droppings that littered the floor and the scattering of bones and fishheads he had sucked clean till they shone.

He didn't recognize Papik and Vivi until they had shouted their names several times into the huge pavilions of his ears. Then he smiled with his black gums and his foxy little eyes lit up.

"You are the son of Ernenek who was a big noise on the ice?" he creaked with his old man's voice.

"It is not impossible," said Papik.

"Somebody remembers your father's arrival with a sledful of bear hams in this village!"

"Game is getting scarcer," Papik said guiltily.

Siorakidsok was outraged. "What? No bear hams?"

"We have problems. That's why we came. You must help us get a male son."

"So there are some intelligent Men left—who know where to turn for help!"

First of all, Siorakidsok insisted on an exploratory examination of Vivi. He ordered her to step closer and penetrated her with his finger.

"You are tickling me!" she blushed.

"Don't ruin her!" said Papik, worried.

"Hee, hee!" the old man cackled, grinning from ear to ear. "An angakok is trying to find out if it's a boy or a girl."

He went on cackling and wiggling his finger in Vivi, who couldn't have been more embarrassed. Until Papik stamped his foot and demanded the verdict.

Siorakidsok was irked. "The spirits won't be rushed!" Pouting, he terminated the medical examination and licked his finger. "It tastes like a girl. Unless it's a boy. The Moon Man has not yet decided. An angakok will visit him on your behalf, if you'll procure what is needed."

More than their ability to predict the weather and cure diseases, it is their capacity to fly through space and consult the Moon Man that establishes the angakoks' prestige in the family of Men—the Moon Man being responsible, of course, for all things related to pregnancies and births.

"We'll enlist the villagers' help," Papik said.

Although these words failed to break through the old ear-drums, yet Siorakidsok knew exactly what Papik had said. An angakok didn't get to be four hundred years old without knowing a thing or two.

"The villagers are afraid to help," he piped. "The jealous missionary has convinced them that helping an angakok to the Moon is sinful."

"Then what is the solution?"

Siorakidsok leaned forward and lowered his voice to

a conspiratorial whisper, glancing toward the open door, although there wasn't a soul in sight.

"You must take an angakok to some other settlement, one not yet corrupted by the foreign superstitions. But you'll have to smuggle him out, because the two white men in this village will certainly do everything to keep him here."

"Why?"

"They fear an angakok's power once he's free to communicate with our own spirits."

Papik shifted on his feet. "A Man wanted to visit his sister sometime soon. You remember Ivaloo? She is said to live at Pregnant Mountain. It is not impossible that you will find acceptance there."

"An angakok starts preparing his departure—against the machinations of the white men!" Siorakidsok announced triumphantly.

Although the air was crisp on the frozen cove, the couple pitched their skin tent over their sled for shelter, not wanting to share Siorakidsok's sordid quarters during their brief stay. On Siorakidsok's advice, they talked to nobody else. According to him, anyone who knew of their plan to smuggle him out of the village might reveal it to the white men, who would then thwart their departure. Besides, the sedentary population consisted mainly of grandmothers, as in most villages. The men had the bad habit of losing their lives in the water or on the ice long before reaching old age, and the few younger people who might still know Vivi were all out hunting or fishing.

The departure, when Siorakidsok had to be spirited out of the village, was a suspenseful moment.

He had ordered Papik and Vivi to prepare a magic ointment—of seal oil and various finely chewed meats

—that would make him invisible to the white men once he coated his face with it from the outside and his stomach from the inside.

When the sled moved past the dwellings with Siorakidsok perched on top of the bundles, no villager paid any attention to it, of course, because it was plainly a departure. But the two white men looked on with undisguised curiosity. They weren't real residents—just two trappers, father and son, who used the village as a base before returning south with their haul of skins.

Papik and Vivi didn't know whether the mysterious ointment was effective, as it was supposed to fool white men only, and in fact they themselves could see Siorakidsok with distressing clarity, all bundled up in his balding dogskins, which they had stuffed for added warmth with some discarded foxmops.

But evidently the magic worked, for the white men made no move to prevent the angakok's departure.

Papik and Vivi had made a clear agreement with Siorakidsok. They would get him to Ivaloo's village that lay beyond the white men's influence and where he might find the recognition an angakok deserved. In return, Siorakidsok, on reaching safe ground, would fly to the Moon Man and try winning him over for their cause.

Papik and Vivi were both far too worldly-wise to believe blindly in any angakok's claims. No thinking man, starting with the founders of great religions, has ever been entirely free of doubts. But they saw no other course of action. And they knew of the white men's angakoks acknowledged inability to influence a coming child's sex, whereas their own angakoks were right at least half the time.

Hope was the ground for the couple's faith.

And their faith, or hope, had to be vast indeed, to make them put up with Siorakidsok, who turned out to be a most trying traveling companion. All the time he clamored for food, but with scarce success, even when he threatened to die, for spite, unless Papik would satisfy him. Papik was unimpressed, and fed him on the same principle as the dogs—just enough to hold his soul glued to his body, since anything more would only enlarge his shrunken stomach and increase future demands.

Vivi dutifully chewed the meats for the toothless guest, but she refused to feed him mouth-to-mouth like a baby, as he persistently requested. He also kept suggesting that she should breast-feed him, asserting that as an angakok he knew how to extract milk from a pregnant woman. As Vivi turned him down, he would sulk.

But soon he would start all over again.

Papik was often tempted to use the old man as dog food. Only fear of his shade and desire for a son stayed his hand. When the first blizzard of fall forced them to erect a shelter, they relegated Siorakidsok to the tunnel, with the pack. When he protested, loudly reminding them that they owed him three-fold respect—as an angakok, as an old man, and as a guest—Papik merely provided him with a rattle with which to call for help if the pack should attack him.

But not even the dogs seemed particularly keen on that scrawny runt, clad in skins of their fellows, and Papik had to intervene only once.

On reaching their destination, a startling discovery made all three of them regret that Siorakidsok had left his former residence.

Pregnant Mountain already had its angakok—and it was somebody of whom Papik and Vivi were so fond that they wouldn't have taken any other into consideration had they only known about it. The person whom the whole settlement regarded as an angakok endowed with mysterious knowledge was Papik's own sister.

The sweet Ivaloo.

10

Ivaloo

The truth of the matter is that the Men want guidance, and if they haven't an angakok, they make one up.

It takes as little as a lucky prediction for a man or a woman to be suspected of possessing supernatural powers, and either further coincidences or else a bit of cunning may turn the assumption into certainty. No one was still alive to remember Siorakidsok's beginnings.

But everybody knew Ivaloo's.

In her case, a correct weather forecast had started it all. She had predicted a blizzard that the hunters had ruled out. Then somebody recalled the case of her miraculous childbirth when she had been living in another settlement, further south, in the village at the cove, where there had been no man for over a year. Except the missionary, of course. And as a carefully brought up girl, Ivaloo had at all times refrained from looking at the moon. Although the missionary himself had determinedly ruled out a miracle, and he was surely an authority on the subject, the villagers had attributed Ivaloo's pregnancy to divine interposition at a time when she had lain unconscious following an excessive intake of the mission's firewater.

Ivaloo herself disclaimed any unusual power. But the more she did, the more credit the villagers gave her for it. The oftener she declared that she had never visited the Moon Man, the surer they were that she flew to him all the time, while they slept.

And that the Moon Man thought highly of her.

Papik and Vivi hadn't seen Ivaloo yet when they learned this. They had stopped at the first hut they reached under Pregnant Mountain to spruce up for the great reunion and gather information. Pregnant Mountain was really an island, but during eleven months of the year only the fish could see that, for it was united to the nearby mainland by the frozen sea crust that lent it the appearance of a giant boulder in a snowy plain.

Papik and Vivi arrived when fall was well advanced, the ocean solid, the air gray and raw, heralding the night. The hut where they had stopped was of the kind the Men build of sod and stones under the bird cliffs after the summer hunting inland, before erecting their winter igloos on the bay ice which, owing to the underlying water, is warmer than the deeply frozen earth.

The hut was occupied by two Men. The younger one was so slinky and languid-eyed that he looked like a woman, only more so. The visitors didn't realize he was a boy until he bared his chest. Papik and Vivi chuckled in a good-natured way. Like everybody else, they had heard of old Noluk and his young companion who sewed him his clothes and carved his kills.

"What about Ivaloo, somebody's sister?" Papik asked, while Vivi knelt at his feet to scrape his boots clean.

"Still waiting for her husband's return," Noluk said.

Papik and Vivi had learned long ago from other sleds that Milak, Ivaloo's husband, hadn't been heard of since going after bears on an ice floe. Three years was a long time to be away bear hunting, at least from a wife's point of view, but it was not unusual. In spring, many Men allow themselves to be carried off on floes by the circular northwest currents that might land them hundreds of miles further south, and they don't find each autumn the proper southeast wind to get back.

Ivaloo had no doubt that Milak would return, no matter how hard all the men were trying to convince her of the contrary. Small wonder. Ivaloo had a pretty face and muscular body, but to their great chagrin she was not the merry kind.

"She smiles at everyone, but laughs with no one," was the way Noluk put it. And then he told of her secret powers.

"An angakok will expose her as an imposter and a fraud!" Siorakidsok shrilly announced after Papik had relayed the news to him by dint of shouting.

Noluk scowled and told Papik: "He should have more respect for his age. Some people might be tempted to use his tongue as bearbait if he slanders Ivaloo."

"Watch your tongue!" Papik warned Siorakidsok. "It is in danger."

Siorakidsok was so upset about the unfair competition that he turned down—believe it or not—the lump of maggoty liver Noluk's companion offered him on a soapstone dish.

Papik was no longer paying attention to the angakok and little to the food.

"Hurry," he told Vivi, who was short of breath by dint of rubbing his boots. "Somebody wants to see his sister."

Brother and sister stood staring for a moment at each other on the threshold of her gloomy abode. A handful of years must have passed since their last encounter.

Ivaloo lived by herself in a hut of turf braced with

whalebones. She was squat of build, a real polar woman, shorter and broader than Vivi. Her round, warm face was still very lovely, but her burnt-almond eyes a bit less vivacious than Papik remembered them. Since becoming Milak's wife, she had let her hair down, in two long tresses held by a headband and falling over her chest in the southern fashion. And instead of shaggy bearhides, she wore the fancy garments she had once derided—of caribou leather trimmed with fox and beads and ribbons.

As soon as she recovered from her surprise, she rushed into Papik's arms, to rub noses and poke cheeks and sniff at his face, cackling and cooing for joy the while.

Only after she had also rubbed noses with Vivi did Ivaloo notice that the package they had carried in on the caribou rug was Siorakidsok, and welcomed him with little cries and deep vows.

"You claim to be an angakok?" Siorkidsok assailed her at once. "You're a false angokok but an authentic fraud!"

Ivaloo replied with her warm smile: "That's what a silly woman keeps telling everybody. But they won't listen. Maybe you can persuade them."

Siorakidsok misunderstood and shouted back: "Don't call me a quack, you quack!"

Meanwhile some people from nearby dwellings had seen the sled and come into the hut, and one man demanded irately on catching Siorakidsok's words:

"Whose dog is this? Kick him out!"

"No, no!" Ivaloo laughed. "Siorakidsok is a very wise angakok. Who can confirm that a silly woman isn't."

"Don't believe her!" Siorakidsok was fighting for his life, and the others had to shout themselves hoarse to make him understand that Ivaloo was on his side.

When he realized that although a mere woman she wielded great influence, he made a neat turnabout. He became all smiles, asserted that he had always sensed Ivaloo's supernatural powers, promised his support, and predicted a brilliant future for her—thus earning everybody's approval.

Except Ivaloo's.

"A silly woman is believed wise just because she has not been wrong a couple of times," she said. "If there is a crumb of sense in her head at all, she owes it to Siorakidsok, who once let her have some of his lice."

It was true. Once when she had expressed her envy for the old angakok's wisdom, he had allowed her to pick a few lice from his scalp, so that they might transmit some of his knowledge to her ignorant little head.

"It is useless to deny an agakok's word!" Siorakidsok shrieked. "Listen, Ivaloo. Somebody has a proposal for you. But first, all visitors go home!"

The visitors went, but Siorakidsok's proposal had to wait. The family dragged his rug, with him on it, to a corner, under the skinned fox carcasses that hung from the ceiling, and started conversing privately, knowing that he couldn't overhear them.

Siorakidsok also knew it and decided to fall asleep.

"Please do not tell me that Milak is sure to come back," Ivaloo started out at once, smiling broadly; a trifle too broadly. "A woman knows that. After all, what's three years and just a bit more?"

She had put snow to melt in a soapstone vessel, adding a pinch of tea leaves from the tundra. This was southern luxury, and Vivi's nostrils fluttered in anticipation.

Papik laughed with one of his short, coarse burst. "Sure! What's a few years for a man who went off on a floe? Eh?" He recalled names and times and places of

Men who had gone bearhunting and returned after many years. Ivaloo listened with a vacant smile, her gaze remote, as if the matter didn't concern her.

"And if Milak does not come back," Papik went on blithely, "plenty of others will be glad to take you. You know how to sew watertight garments, in case a man falls into the water."

Ivaloo kept smiling at nothing and looking toward the winter, and when the drinking snow had melted she started passing the vessel around.

Vivi gulped a big swallow and said bluntly: "A woman has a problem. The child she carries must come out a boy, for it's the last child she will bear. She can't forget the girl that had to die."

"A woman knows how it feels to lose a child," Ivaloo nodded, far away. "And hers was a healthy male son, beginning to walk and talk—a real little man. That loss was much worse."

"Vivi makes too much fuss about that girl," Papik burst in. "After all, she was still so little! And a father didn't strangle her or wring her neck, as some do. He set her out in the gale, still wet from birth, and stuffed her mouth with snow, to make her freeze faster. Meanwhile he held her hands, to reassure her. She didn't even have time to cry, went to sleep almost at once. There is no easier death. A man knows, who more than once came close to freezing. And then we cut off the head of one of our best dogs and left it with the little girl, to guide her to the children's Paradise."

"She has not found the way," Vivi said dully. "She comes back in a mother's dreams, naked and cold. And a woman is not going to set her next birth out on the ice —even if it's a girl."

Papik spat and stamped his foot. "We need a son—a hunter! No one can raise two small children at once. You can't carry more than one in your hood. Outside, a child gets eaten by the dogs or falls into a hole or gets lost."

"What would you do, Ivaloo?" Vivi asked her sister-in-law. "You who are so wise."

"A woman never said it. The others say so."

"It's what the others say that matters. What would you do in my place?"

"If you have faith, you will get a boy," said Ivaloo, remembering her early Christian indoctrination and forgetting how disastrously it had turned out.

"But what if it's a girl?" Vivi urged.

Ivaloo remained silent.

"Answer!"

Ivaloo didn't. In the silence, a call from the forgotten corner startled the trio. Siorakidsok had woken up and demanded to be heard.

"Listen, Ivaloo! An angakok will risk another space flight to enlist the Moon Man's aid for Vivi's coming birth—but on one condition." And he paused for effect.

"What is it?" Ivaloo asked.

"If an angakok cames back alive from his dangerous trip, you shall impress upon those helpless clods that believe in you that he is the one they must obey, revere, and feed—with nothing but the best. And while he's on the moon, he will also ask the whereabouts of your husband." And before Ivaloo could recover her breath, he delivered the clincher: "Whereafter he will reveal to you the real secrets of the angakoks."

"Including how to travel to the moon?" inquired Papik.

"That first of all."

"How can you find out about Milak?" Ivaloo asked, breathless. "The Moon Man is only concerned with pregnancies."

"Humbug! From his lofty heights, he sees everything. But you know it takes the proper gifts—besides skill and experience—to worm the required information out of him." Siorakidsok leaned forward and inquired anxiously: "Will you be able to procure them?"

"It is not impossible."

Of course, the Power that rules pregnancies is full of mischief—ask any girl—and no effort must be spared to curry his good graces.

So Ivaloo made the round of the dwellings, scrounging what delicate viands she could get that might contribute to the success of Siorakidsok's moon trip—bird slime, seal guts, meats so long dead that they were alive with maggots, and even that supreme treat of all: a whole sealskin crammed with blubber and unplucked little seabirds. When it has been buried for a whole year, away from the sun to slow the process of decay, the contents amalgamate into a violet paste that has the flavor of cheese and the fragrance of a corpse. No Man, and surely not even the one in the moon, has ever tasted anything better.

The other women helped Ivaloo to masticate these dainties, as the Moon Man, being very old, is toothless. But when she presented the result of their concerted efforts, Siorakidsok sent her back for more. Twice.

"The spirits are not what they used to be," he sighed. "The Moon Man gets more difficult every year."

When Siorakidsok was satisfied at last, a little lean-to was thrown up out of sight of the village, and the fearless angakok was locked in it with sufficient goodies to make even the crankiest Moon Man happy. A hole had been left in the roof for the soul to escape, and for three turns of the sun, the duration of a space trip, nobody dared approach the site, for no common mortal may find out how an angakok leaves earth and returns to it.

On pain of immediate and horrible death.

At the term's end, the family and a gaggle of village women flocked to the angakok's lean-to, eager to hear the latest news from the moon.

A surprise awaited them.

Siorakidsok had indeed found his way back to earth, but he hadn't survived the ordeal. A real pity, for the victuals had been consumed to the last crumb, proving that the Moon Man must have welcomed them and provided the requested answers.

But this turned out to be a rash conclusion. A closer look revealed that the old angakok had devoured at least some of the tidbits himself—and wished he hadn't. His scrawny belly was spattered with the evidence.

Whatever Siorakidsok's last secrets, he was taking them along into the afterworld.

Not even Ivaloo could tell with certainty what had occurred out there in space. Perhaps the Moon Man had not found the offerings from earth to his liking, and flung them back at its ambassador—who hadn't had the heart to waste them. Beyond such surmises, there was one certainty: the Moon Man must be angry.

Which boded ill for Papik's family.

The continuous urgency of the present didn't allow worrying about the future anymore than brooding over the past. First of all, Siorakidsok's body had to be disposed of. The safest way out was to abandon him to the animals. By destroying him, they would make sure that he couldn't come back in exactly the same shape as before, causing mischief.

Since touching a corpse with bare hands is lethal, and any gloves used for the purpose have to be thrown away afterward, the villagers dragged the carcass out into the open by a trace looped around the ankles. On that occasion they discovered that his mangy hides had not been the angakok's only possession. While he was being dragged, a small satchel fell from him—containing all the teeth the old man had lost in his life. Then they dropped the carcass into a ravine, muttering "good riddance" as they watched it tumble from rock to rock. Whereafter, they all hastened to exorcise the dead man's shade, whose animosity against the living surely no one could overestimate.

For the older a man, the fiercer his resentment for having to quit this best of all worlds.

Exhausted from the ceremonies, everybody then went to sleep, practicing for the impending winter.

It was the time of year when, during each turn of the sun, the darkness already lasts longer than the daylight. On awakening, the community was shocked to discover that Siorakidsok's body had disappeared, though there were no traces of animals at the bottom of the ravine. No one dared venture down to make sure. Everybody was convinced that the angakok had come back to life and was lurking in the shadows.

Waiting to strike.

If all the others were merely apprehensive, Vivi and Papik were terrified. They would be the first targets of Siorakidsok's wrath, being responsible for his fatal trip. So the villagers resented the couple's presence and consulted Ivaloo.

As the wise woman she was, Ivaloo reached the inevitable verdict: Papik and Vivi must depart at once, for the common good. But when she went to look for them, the couple had already broken camp.

They had evidently reached the same conclusion and left Pregnant Mountain without tearful good-bys.

11

The Moon Man's Revenge

It was spring and they were traveling along the coastal ice by the two granite hills known as Devil's Tits when Vivi brought forth her child.

A husband can shorten a woman's labor. While she kneels over the hole gouged in the ice, he can put his arms around her from behind and help her press. But Papik had waddled off after a stray caribou and Vivi was on her own and without shelter when the pangs started, and all she could do was upend the sled in the way of a windbreak.

Experience had taught her to breathe in deeply with each cramp and then contract her abdominal muscles in order to expedite the expulsion. Since nothing could be done against the pain, she might as well get it over with in a hurry.

Just when she thought she couldn't bear it any longer and the world was beginning to darken before her eyes, the child's head popped out, relieving her. As the rest of the baby followed quickly, the head hit the ice hole with a thud, but Vivi was confident that it was resilient or clever enough to absorb the shock.

What was worrying Vivi was not the newborn's head. She had kept a fine oyster shell handy for cutting the

90

child free—the same she had used for her baby girl, but now she couldn't find it. Bending forward, gritting her teeth against the flash of pain, she delivered herself by gnawing through the umbilical cord, which for all its softness was surprisingly tough.

A good omen for the newborn's resilience.

Fearing the freezing gale, she postponed licking clean the dripping bundle of pink flesh she had produced and slipped it at once under her jacket, against her skin. Then she pulled up her trousers and stretched herself out, waiting for the afterbirth. As she hadn't cleaned the baby, she hadn't been able to determine its sex.

Or perhaps she preferred postponing the discovery.

The pangs announcing the afterbirth soon followed. She had fastened the dogs on the other side of the sled at the first sign of labor. By now they had got wind of the blood and were getting restless, though Karipari was growling for order and charging the unruliest.

Vivi was glad she hadn't mislaid the dog stick as well.

By the time she felt the soft heat of the placenta on her thighs, two dogs had broken their bonds and came drooling over her. Many women ate their placenta hot from the womb, not only because they ate anything that would go down and stay there, but also because it was vital matter, believed to relax the nerves and even to assuage the pain, besides strengthening the body. But Vivi didn't feel like eating anything, and let the two dogs have hers. As they fell to, their companions redoubled their efforts to break their fetters.

Vivi wished Papik would come back.

He came home dead tired. Bent forward, he was dragging his kill by a thong held over his shoulder—a caribou calf that was lining the ice with a red mark.

Now he should be allowed to drop on his back and let his wife take over. It was her duty to flense the kill and

carve it and feed her husband and watch his belly ex-
pand like a balloon, while she kept dropping choice
morsels into his furnace until they came out of his nose.

Not this time.

Papik squatted on the ice and stared at Vivi's figure.
The bulge that had been low in her trousers when he left
had moved up to her parka during his absence.

"The child?" he asked. She nodded and he urged:
"Well?!"

"A boy," she said quietly.

Papik bounced to his feet, his weariness forgotten,
and his whoops of joy silenced the huskies that had started whining and barking at the sight of the kill. Then he
rubbed noses with Vivi, and she lifted her parka and let
him steal a glance at the little face.

"He is blond! And his eyes are light—besides a little
crossed!"

"They may become blue in time," Vivi said.

Papik's jaw dropped. "A white man's son? From
Cape Misery?"

"It is not impossible."

Neither was it impossible that Papik would have preferred a son from his own loins. But any son was better
than a girl, and he was overjoyed that his wish had been
fulfilled at last.

Here was one little white man who was going to become a real man.

The baby wasn't much uglier than other newborns,
with a puffy face and a wrinkled brow. At first glance,
apart from the light coloring of hair and eyes, it looked
much similar to the newborn Men, owing to the Asiatic
shape of its eyes—Vivi's most apparent legacy.

The baby had started to cry when the parka was lifted, baring its toothless gums, and Papik laughed recall-
ing the incident that had marked his own birth. Nobody
had informed his parents that nature delivered the hu-

man beings without teeth, unlike all the animals they knew. The blow was cruel, the solution inescapable. Poor little Papik, a toothless misfit, would have to be set out to die, for his own good. The experienced grandmother had saved him just in time, revealing the truth —before going out to die on the ice of her own free will.

Not to be a further burden to a couple that now had a child to rear.

It was fortunate that Papik's weariness had been dispelled by the good news, for now he had many things to do and all of them urgent. The truant dogs had to be hobbled, the tent of skins had to be pitched over the sled so that Vivi might safely lick the child clean before smearing it with blubber, and the kill had to be flensed and carved before it hardened. In his enthusiasm he ran around in circles, trying to do all things at once, until the wind swept away the tent before it was fastened, calling for a sturdier igloo made of snow.

But as he was about to start on the construction, sudden exhaustion struck him down, and he fell asleep with his face on the snowcrust. That always caused a stiff jaw, and Vivi pushed the handle of a knife under his cheek. Then, unable to stand the uncertainty one moment longer, she lifted her parka and inspected the baby.

A girl.

"A silly woman has decided to call him Ootuniah," Vivi was saying.

"Why not Ernenek, like somebody's father?" asked Papik.

"It is not impossible that a silly woman knows what to do. She has whispered all our ancestors' names into his ear, so any one of them may have entered him, giving him their knowledge. But Ootuniah was a silly woman's grandfather. He appeared in her last few sleeps, shivering. His name has not yet found a body to keep it warm. That's why she will call this child Ootuniah."

A soul looks like a little person, with wings added. Bereft of its body, it will enter the first available newborn. A name looks much like a soul, but smaller still. When the body dies, its name is condemned to float in the cold, lonesome and miserable, until someone assigns it to a new being that will keep it warm. Souls and names are sexless—they can dwell indifferently in females or males in humans or animals.

"We named one of our bitches Ernenek, for your father," Vivi reminded Papik.

"A bitch that went astray."

"But may still be alive. Has your father appeared in your dreams, wretched and cold?"

"Not lately," said Papik.

"Then his name is safe and warm."

So was the little family in the igloo Papik had erected on awakening. Building in the gale had not been easy without Vivi's help. She was still a bit shaken from childbirth, and she wanted to keep the baby warm against her skin.

For the first time, nothing was missing from one of the couple's igloos.

There was the drinking block sealing the tunnel. The snow couch covered with hides. The spear and harpoon stuck in the vault to form a drying rack. The lamp with the flickering flame reflected by the circular wall. The soapstone bowl placed above it, in case anybody should thirst for melted snow. The vessel of excavated ice in which the urine for washing was kept. The meat placed to rot in the warmth of the lamp, and some more under the couch spread. Somewhere against the wall, the bow and arrows, the garment scrapers, and the house knife, which was circular so as to require only a movement of the wrist and not of the elbow, which would be awkward in the cramped quarters.

Each of their igloos had been exactly like this one, following an architecture dictated by necessity and therefore immutable. But now something was added that completed the picture.

Little Ootuniah.

The child's groin was still protected by the foxtail, for according to Vivi the umbilical wound had not healed yet. Papik's eyes bulged the first time he saw the buttocks.

"Where is the spot?" he cried in panic, for the new-born Men are supposed to have the blue Mongolic mark at the base of the spine—if they are boys.

"He is a white man's son—that's why he has no spot."

Vivi's calm answer reassured him. The baby was all mouth and belly, and Papik had the time of his life watching it suckle and slurp and burp in Vivi's arms. She refused to surrender it, asserting it needed the mother's warmth. Papik was merely allowed to tickle the little nose and bulging cheeks, trying to make the baby laugh until it cried, and to let some seal oil or some thoroughly insalivated meat cuds trickle into the toothless little cave. And if, carried away by his enthusiasm, he dropped too much food at once, the clever baby surrendered it all, throwing it up together with the milk.

Feeling keenly the responsibilities of fatherhood, Papik decided it would be safer not to travel at once. They no longer needed an angakok's advice. And although most wildlife had already started burrowing into the ground, he remained above it, roaming the snowy coast in search of game.

The top of the world had turned gray and Ootuniah's

eyes had turned blue and could follow a moving finger when the inevitable came to pass.

On awakening from a nap, Papik had a sudden intuition: it occurred to him that Vivi wasn't as happy as he had expected. He bounced off the couch, and while Vivi was still rubbing the dreams out of her eyes, he stripped the foxtail off the baby's crotch. Then, remaining on his knees, he gaped in horror at what the Black Raven that created Men has not created to be gaped at in horror.

Although Vivi had never been struck in all her life, she instinctively lifted an arm to protect her face.

But Papik merely mumbled, brokenhearted: "The Moon Man's revenge."

"A silly woman wants to keep her!"

"You know it can't be," Papik said dully. "Soon somebody will be old. And a boy must grow some before he can hunt. Then only can we raise a girl, too—if you still want one. But first a hunter."

"A mother wants to keep Ootuniah." And Vivi clasped the baby to her chest.

"You know it can't be." Papik's disappointment was as deep as his joy had been high. "Now it will be harder than if we had done it at once. For her, too. Your fault."

Suddenly Vivi struck out.

Her eyes swelling with tears, she seized Ootuniah by the ankles and slammed her against Papik, who got hold of the baby and closed her in his arms. Vivi flung herself down on the couch then and broke into sobs. But she jumped up almost at once, her eyes red, her body shaking, snatched Ootuniah from Papik and cried:

"Then do it now!"

In a frenzy she dived into the tunnel, shoving the screaming Ootuniah out ahead of her. Outside, she laid the naked girl down on the wind crust and stifled her cries by stuffing her mouth with snow. Papik turned away, but Vivi spun him around.

"Watch!" she screamed into his face.

"A man told you—we should have done it at once!"

Vivi clutched his chin and forced him to face the child. Ootuniah was no longer crying, but munching the mouthful of snow with delight, smiling and cooing.

"Look at her! It's my last child you'll see die. For a woman will never laugh again. Never! She's had a belly-ful of men!"

Papik frowned. Little Ootuniah had never looked more endearing, kicking out with gusto, smiling and bubbling with her mouth full of melting snow. Unless it was Vivi's threatened strike that prompted Papik to think twice.

"There may be something we can do," he mused.

Vivi caught her breath. This was the first inkling that he was not immovable, and she charged headlong into the breach. Frenziedly she rubbed snow on the naked baby, who gasped as if she had been knifed.

Papik seized Vivi by the shoulders. "What are you doing? Has a wolverine bitten you?" Vivi freed herself and flung more snow upon Ootuniah. As the snow melting on the baby's skin was quickly turning to ice, Papik hastened to carry her back indoors.

When Vivi followed, her cheeks were gray with frozen tears, her eyes rimmed with rime.

"A man just had a thought," Papik told her, scratching the ice crust from the little body. "The white men's taboo against killing applies to baby girls, too. Let's bring them Ootuniah."

"Perhaps they don't want her."

"Why don't you listen? They can't set her out to die. It's taboo."

The full meaning of Papik's words sank in but slowly. Vivi's tears were still in spate, melting the ice on her cheeks, when she silenced Ootuniah with her hot breast.

"We'll leave her with the one who laughed with you," Papik said. "Who?" He had been too proud, besides too tactful, to ask that question before.

Vivi pondered the answer well. "It could be Tor. Yes! Ootuniah would be in good hands with Tor and Birgit." Her eyes lit up. "They are well-bred, good-hearted people, considering they are foreigners. Especially Birgit. She will be delighted if we present her with Tor's little girl."

And with this decision, the lost laughter found its way back to their igloo.

12

The Son

They know two methods of birth control.

The first is prolonged lactation, which in the women of the Men usually prevents the return of the menses and the state of fertility. Many mothers can nurse a child up into adult age and remain barren, to be spared the one alternative at their disposal.

Infanticide.

Vivi and Papik had no such problem now. After their resolve to palm off Ootuniah on the white men, begetting a son had once more become urgent. So Vivi weaned her little girl early, increasing the trickles of seal oil from her finger and the meat cuds from her mouth. Presently lactation ebbed; but it took a great many sleeps before menstruation returned, and with it her ability to conceive.

Little Ootuniah throve on her carnivorous diet, bolstered with throbbing mussels and shrimps from the seals' stomachs, blood bubbling with life, and fish eyes still able to see. And she could play with a toy her mother had hopefully been carrying around on her many childless journeys—a rattle made from three dried ptarmigan stomachs, inflated like little balloons, containing the last grains the birds had swallowed, and providing the lovely noise that causes every baby's eyes to pop with wonder and delight.

It was a happy igloo.

Frequent laughter reverberated from the blood-spattered snow wall as they wintered on the sea ice close to shore. The proud father crowed with glee when he played ball with Vivi, using that unbreakable doll that was learning early to smile a lot.

He could have drifted into a winter sleep, allowing his body to live on the fat capital accumulated under his skin during the summer. But since babies were not made to hibernate, he stayed mostly awake. There was always enough to do in an igloo for a real man. First of all he could laugh with his wife. Then he could pluck the scant hairgrowth off his face, to avoid accumulation of moisture that would turn to frost. Repair his gear. Beautify his spear and harpoon with pretty carvings, for animals prefer being slain by attractive weapons rather than plain ones, as who wouldn't. And meantime he made sure that little Ootuniah got her fill every time she screamed for it, which was often, for she still was all mouth and belly, her only activities consisting of crying and giggling, eating and eliminating.

Or he slapped blubber on his face and crawled out to reconnoiter the winter.

So it was that in the deepest night he spotted a bear skulking over the ice under the silent stars. The somber coastline was sharply emblazoned against the glittering canopy in which the North Star blazed supreme, and the icebergs and islets cast blue shadows on the pearly seafields. The bear's shaggy coat, in daylight always yellow by contrast with the ice, looked white in the starshine.

Papik let out a couple of seals' bellows to attrack the beast's attention. It was far too cold out for discarding the bear suit in order to look like a seal. The threadbare carpet of snow crunched under his soft boots. Other evidences of very low temperature were the wind stillness and the heady scent of ozone that he believed descended from the stars, for it was always heaviest when the sky was ablaze with them. He exhaled with force, experimentally, and heard the blast of the moisture in his breath as it froze instantly.

It was not warm.

Man and bear started circling warily, the vapor from their lungs shimmering, silvered by the starlight. Papik reflected that bears were no longer what they used to be when he hit this one on the nose with a clump of ice, and the animal slunk away, casting side-glances to make sure that there were no witnesses of its cowardice around. Papik trailed it, hoping to provoke it into a head-on attack. He couldn't block its retreat without the help of dogs, and as usual he had none to spare.

The bear shuffled calmly along the coast, until it caught a scent and started burrowing. Nearing with caution, Papik saw it lift from the frosting a wolverine as big as a husky, drugged with sleep, now bleeding from the neck. As Papik lunged forward with raised spear, the bear abandoned its catch.

Papik took over.

Wolverine is not only the maddest and bloodthirstiest creature but also the cleverest and bravest; by comparison, man and bear are clumsy clods. Papik had never before succeeded in bagging one, but had often been, like everyone else, the victim of the wolverine's vicious mischief. And when he brought that one home, he was prouder than if he had felled a male bear.

While the thick fur would make the warmest parka for a child, the meat turned out to be inferior, as Papik had expected from such a wicked animal, but he ate the liver and the heart, to assimilate the wolverine's courage. As to the brain, he considered that Vivi needed it more than he did, and let her eat a generous share. Vivi made Ootuniah sample it too, wanting her to grow up wily and sharp-witted, able to cope with the mad world of the white men that was awaiting her. They made sure to bury the jaws in the ice, for the mere touch of the wolverine's teeth could transmit its rabies.

Papik had never felt more confident than after eating that wolverine's vital parts. He was sure that his guardian angel had returned to stay. Vivi smiled and laughed again. Ootuniah was an endless source of merriment. They were no longer threatened by Siorakidsok's shade, nor by the white men's taboos and punishments. They had to cope merely with normal hazards—icequakes and icebreaks, freezing in the winter, drowning in the summer, starvation, bears, and their own spirits' capriciousness.

Which left every Man worth his name an even chance to see another season.

Papik's optimism seemed justified when at the rise of day Vivi found herself once again warm with child.

Although they were a long way from Cape Misery, they made very little headway during the summer—a good season for hunting but a poor one for traveling. They had to procure food and put on weight. With the result that in fall they were still so far from the destination that it was preferable sitting out another winter on the sea ice rather than trekking overland, where it was too cold to dwell, let alone to travel with a baby in Vivi's hood and another in her belly.

The presence of little Ootuniah lent their winter igloo a novel charm. When the ocean rumbled underfoot, gently rocking their little abode, Papik worried about the baby girl—in case the crust should break open and engulf him, her provider. When he ventured out in the dark, the beacon of the little blister of snow and ice, glowing in the distance, warmed him as if he were safe inside, because he knew that Ootuniah was. He was grateful to Vivi for having induced him to spare that little life.

And yet, when necessity demanded that he risk it, risk it he did.

"How is it possible?" he marveled when Vivi told him that they were out of food.

It seemed only one short sleep ago that they thawed out a whole seal he had stored in the ice a few years back—not a very large one, to tell the truth. And to tell the full truth, Vivi's new pregnancy, now much advanced, had trebled her appetite and, unexplainably, doubled Papik's. Not to mention the dogs, who seemed to grow hungrier the less they were fed.

It gave rise to a domestic squabble to remember.

"A man kills himself trying to hunt in the night!" Papik faced Vivi with a belligerent stance. "And meanwhile he sharpens weapons, repairs harnesses, feeds the team! And when he wants to take a little nap, a wife says: 'Guess what? The larder is empty!'"

He imitated Vivi's voice and manner very poorly indeed, and she resented it.

"A woman happens to be eating a bit more, but why?" she lashed back, arms akimbo. "Because a greedy bear wanted his laughs, and now she carries a child that's devouring her belly! Besides, she uses up her teeth on her husband's boots, melts his snow, carves his kills, trims the wick, chews Ootuniah's food! She frets her fingers to the bone making needles and sewing clothes! She breaks her back scraping skins! And what does she get? Criticism!"

"A man is making a discovery!" Papik's big chest was heaving. "He's been tricked into marrying a toothless, tailless seal cow instead of a woman! Always whimpering, never willing to laugh! But it's his own fault. Picking a wife from the ridiculous South—a water woman!"

That did it.

Vivi could shrug off personal insults, like the obvious lie that she was never willing to laugh, but no aspersions on the South. She grabbed hold of the nearest object—a boot that hung from the drying rack, as yet stiff with frost—and took to pelting Papik with it, right and left and right and left and more and again, grinning in anger. The first blow surprised him and bloodied his nose, but he warded off the next ones by putting up his arms and trying to squirm out of range.

Among the Men, as among the wild animals, only the female beats her mate. The male never beats the female. Occasionally he kills her; but that is all. Vivi's persistent and vain endeavors to reshape his features eventually turned Papik's anger into laughter. And as there was little room for retreat, he stumbled backward and fell upon Ootuniah who was on the couch, arousing her obstreperous protests.

The little girl won the fight, hands down.

The exertion had increased the couple's appetite, aggravating the food problem instead of solving it, and Papik burned some of their last blubber as bait, removing the ptarmigan skin from the air vent in the roof to let the fragrance escape. If this trick was not guaranteed to attract bears, it was guaranteed to chill the igloo and eventually freeze its dwellers. But they had to chance it.

Waiting for the bears, they dozed off, until a barking of dogs jarred them back into alertness. They had slept long, for the boots on the rack were almost dry. Papik crawled out into the night.

And a bear it was—hungry enough to defy the dogs, not enough to approach the man, not even when Papik played dead on the ice. Curiosity drew it a little closer, but its diffidence kept it out of range.

A man could feed a bear a blubber ball primed with a whalebone coil that sprang open when the blubber melted in the stomach. But then he had to trail his quarry until it was gutted of all strength, sometimes for several turns, and Papik wasn't wearing enough brawn and fat for a long chase in that temperature. As for planting a greased blade in the ground for the quarry to lick, cutting its own tongue to ribbons and bleeding to death, it worked with wolves and sometimes even with a fox.

Bear was too smart for that.

This one was eyeing Papik placidly, seated on its haunches, impervious to the cold. Bear was the only animal that could winter on the polar ice and weather any blizzard without a shelter, its igloo being only for the cubs.

When Papik felt the frost slowing his limbs, he returned home and ordered Vivi to dress Ootuniah.

"You are not going to use her as bait!" Vivi cried, terrified.

"Dress her! Before the bear goes fishing."

Ootuniah knew the outside world only from the vantage point of her mother's hood. When she found herself for the first time abandoned on the great ice, lying under the stars, without so much as a familiar dog face by her, she voiced her indignation stentorianly, kicking and punching.

Spear in hand, Papik had stretched out within throwing range.

Curiosity over the shrieking, tossing bundle of baby sealskin and wolverine hide finally overcame the animal's diffidence. But when it shambled close to sniff, Ootuniah was on the trajectory and Papik couldn't throw his spear.

He waited for the bear to move, knowing that such a wise hunter would first circle an unfamiliar prey. But the instant the bear had exposed its flank, they were both startled by a cry from the tunnel—and Vivi came charging out in succor of her young, eyes flashing, clutching the axe.

In the time it took Papik to glance at her, the bear had picked up Ootuniah and turned tail.

Papik hurled his spear at once, blindly, entrusting it to his guardian angel. The angel didn't miss. Not quite. The flinthead traversed a rear tendon and the bear bucked and slowed, hampered by the heavy weapon that the hind paw was dragging, but holding on to its catch. Papik waddled in pursuit and Vivi waddled after Papik, shrieking like a seal gull and brandishing the axe.

The bear bucked and kicked until it had shed the spear, then dropped its catch to lick the wound between one bounce and the next. Running and slipping and scrambling back to his feet, Papik recovered his spear, caught up with the bear which had started hobbling on three legs, paralyzed its hindquarters by lancing its spine and plunged the knife into its gullet.

Ootuniah had stopped crying the instant the bear had picked her up. Now she was tittering at the two big faces that were anxiously inspecting her. She had had the time of her life.

Not so her mother.

As soon as she had ascertained that her daughter was well, Vivi doubled over, pressing her stomach, as if sick or in pain. She was both. The fright had shocked her womb into action, and she was in labor.

Papik helped her into the igloo.

The newborn had everything that makes a Man fit for life on the ice. A stocky body and blunt hands designed to retain heat, large jaws prepared for strong teeth, close-lying ears and flat features to foil frostbite, the Mongolic fold over deep-set slit-eyes to reduce the exposed surface, narrow nose channels to forewarm the inhaled air. And the base of the spine exhibited the blue racial spot—hallmark of every true Man's son.

This baby deserved being named Ernenek, after Papik's own father.

For the time being, he was still as tender and bloody as the womb that had dropped him headfirst into the ice hole. After Vivi had licked him clean and smeared him with blubber, she let him lie on the couch wearing nothing but the foxtail in his crotch. Constant exposure couldn't start too soon, toughening the skin and building up the thick callus between the core and the surface that would shield him from frost, and not only from frost, like fur protects animals.

When at the first hint of day the family prepared to move on, a problem had to be solved—where to keep this second child. Or where to keep the first.

If little Ernenek couldn't do without his mother's trundle hood, Ootuniah also needed protection, for she was at the toddling stage and making the most of it. So at the moment of departure, Vivi presented Papik with a trundle hood she had sewn for him on the sly.

Papik greeted it with derisive laughter, and announced to Vivi and the world that she must have been bitten by a wolverine if she believed that a man would allow himself to be saddled with a baby, like a common woman.

Vivi was too busy to listen. When she had packed the bundles and dressed the children, she slung little Ernenek on her own back and handed Ootuniah to Papik. He gaped at his son, at his wife, at her daughter, and at the dogs.

Then he tucked Ootuniah into his brand new trundle hood, grumbling under his breath.

Papik's main worry as they sledged over the whiteness was lest anyone should see him trundling an infant on his back and spread the news.

"There is nobody around anywhere," Vivi would point out, to reassure him.

But in vain. Papik had noticed that his dogs were already leering at him disrespectfully, and he clobbered them mercilessly, to forestall any insubordination. But what really frightened him was the thought that some seal might report his degradation to the other sea creatures who, noble souls that they were, would certainly refuse to be caught by such a hen-pecked husband.

A warm spring and early breakup of the sea ice marooned the growing family on the wrong side of land. Turning the draft dogs into pack dogs and trekking on foot, each trundling a child, was a mode of traveling that didn't appeal to a polar couple. So they pitched their tent and stayed put for one more season of inland hunting and trapping, waiting for the sea to freeze over.

Thus another brief summer went by.

When Papik was out chasing musk ox or caribou and Vivi did her doubled household chores with little Ernenek in her hood, Ootuniah had to be tied to a stake, to be out of harm's way. For good measure she was given a stick taller than she was and taught to smack it firmly on the nose of every dog that came sniffing at her juicy flesh.

Until the pack had learned not only to love the masters' daughter but also to respect her.

Filling the two children's stomachs took up a good part of Vivi's time. To keep her milk in tide and prevent the return of the dreaded state of fertility, she had put Ootuniah back on her breast, cutting down on the meat cuds.

Papik tried meanwhile to make sure that his son received the proper education. Already before the Mon-

golic spot had faded from the boy's back, his father
would take him on his knees each time he wept, and
command: "Be tough! Don't cry!"—as his own father
used to do with him. But the imperious tone and the
scowl hanging over him like a thunderstorm would terri-
fy the child, fanning his discontent.

Until Papik couldn't help but laugh, and postponed
his educational efforts.

Papik wasn't happier than Vivi about the prospect of
parting from Ootuniah.

Ernenek already showed considerable personality, especially in suckling, trying to squeeze blood besides milk
out of his mother's nipple with his budding teeth, so she
had to stick a bone between his gums lest she be
maimed. But Ootuniah was more—already a full-
fledged little person. However, the couple had become
ever more convinced, as the children grew and with
them their demands, that one of the two had to go. So it
was with a sigh of relief in spite of great sadness in their
hearts that they reached Cape Misery before winter's
end.

They halted in sight of Tor's and Birgit's trading post
and spruced Ootuniah up for the meeting with her future parents.

13

The Search

They were sitting in the trading post. The greeting ceremonies were over. Tor's and Birgit's welcome had been warm, their congratulations for the couple's offspring lavish. Ernenek was slumbering in his trundle hood, sucking his thumb, and Ootuniah was playing with her mother's visiting boots, while the four adults traded compliments and smiles.

"Your little Ootuniah is wonderful!" Birgit assured the proud couple, and Tor added: "A real beauty."

"You may have her!" Papik beamed. But not wanting to humiliate his hosts with a gift, he added: "We take some of your steel knives in exchange, and maybe a pack of tea."

"A silly woman likes tea," Vivi confessed.

"We don't trade children in this store," said Tor.

"Vivi may have tea as a present," Birgit added, not afraid to cut in on her husband's decision in public. "We were both very fond of her while she worked for us. Isn't it so, Tor?"

"Of course she can have some tea!" Tor boomed.

"We don't want presents," said Papik. "It wasn't easy bringing a little girl up together with the boy. So you should give us something in exchange. Anything. What?"

Tor looked vaguely alarmed. "Nothing."

"It's a deal!" Papik got up and plunked Ootuniah on the counter.

"Look, we don't take little girls," Tor said with an uncertain smile.

"If a worried mother may dare speak," Vivi said, "you once said that you exchange anything in your store —even an old wife for two young ones."

"That was a joke!"

"You know a little girl can't travel with us," Papik said. "Since we also have a little boy. So you must take her."

While Tor was one big brown bear of a man, Birgit was a big blonde she-bear of a woman, and just as suspicious.

"Why," she asked pointedly, "should we, of all people, take your girl?"

Papik snickered and turned to Vivi: "Shall we tell?"

"Let's," Vivi snickered back, blushing behind her sleeve.

"Because Tor is the father," Papik said.

Tor turned red and Birgit white. For a while, only the muffled giggles of the northern couple were audible. Birgit seemed frozen, although it was very warm, as evidenced by the sweat on Tor's brow.

"Remember? When Vivi worked here," Papik put in helpfully.

"Little Ootuniah is very dear to us," Vivi added. "We don't like losing her. But we are glad we leave her in good hands."

Birgit wasn't listening. She glared at Tor, who was swallowing hard. Then she said something in their own tongue, he answered, and soon their conversation sounded very lively and unfriendly.

"Are they not happy to get Ootuniah?" Vivi asked Papik in a whisper.

"If they don't want her, they don't deserve her!"

"Perhaps they are crazy. In that case it would be dangerous leaving them Ootuniah."

"Then what shall we do with her?"

Vivi pondered, ignoring her hosts' noise, before speaking: "Who said that Tor is the father?"

"You."

"A silly woman may have erred. Would she laugh with such a vulgar old man? It must have been someone else."

Papik scratched his head. "You don't remember?"

"It was so long ago. Now don't start barking and smashing things. There was no time to ask you. Remember that. You were in a hurry to get a son."

"Well, who did you laugh with?"

"Maybe Lars. A woman sometimes brought his house in order. He has no wife to tell him what to do and to turn down his child."

"Let's go to Lars!"

Lars, a shy young man with blond locks, representing the white men's government, housed in a wooden cabin painted yellow on the outside and papered with old newspapers on the inside. He seemed surprised to see Vivi, embarrassed to meet her husband, and dumfounded on being presented with a baby daughter. He hoped he hadn't heard right, since his knowledge of the language was very scant, and to help matters he called Tor —which didn't help matters at all.

While waiting for Tor, Vivi sauntered around the room, curious about the many mysterious or superfluous objects that always cluttered a white man's quarters. Two yellow flowers were growing in a pot. Vivi plucked them, handed one to Papik and munched the other herself. Men had not only a right but an obligation to help themselves to the foods they saw when they went visiting, in token of appreciation, and those flowers were the only edibles around. She didn't let the children taste any; their innocent little stomachs were still too tender for vegetables.

Tor wasn't at his best when he arrived. In the Arctic, few white people are on emerging from a domestic quarrel. He looked even more confused when he learned that Vivi now attributed Ootuniah's fathership to someone else.

"How come?" he scowled, as if he resented the shift as a personal insult.

Vivi smiled. "Whoever gives me meat is my father."

Tor consulted Lars in their own tongue and reported: "First of all Lars is very annoyed because you ate his flowers. It took him a year to grow them, with seeds and earth he had brought at great expense from below the tree line. As to your child, he says he's about to go back home to get married, and the young woman who's been waiting for him would surely start shouting if he showed up with a little daughter. But he will give you a nice present, and I myself will contribute, if you get out of town quietly."

Papik sniffed at the offer. "We don't want presents, but a father for our little girl."

"We can't help you," Tor said, hardening.

"There was another white man here, in the house where children sit," Vivi said.

"You mean Gaah, the teacher?"

"Yes. Gaah."

"He has been replaced," Tor said.

"If the teacher laughed with Vivi," said Papik, "the child belongs to the teacher—even if it's a new one." Tor didn't seem to follow this line of reasoning, and Papik spat angrily at his feet and said: "If you leave us

Ootuniah, it's like letting her die—and that's taboo for you!"

Tor got angry too. "Remember, Papik: if you let this child die, you'll be punished!"

Vivi requested Papik's permission to voice her view.

"A silly woman would like to see this teacher just the same," she said then. "Perhaps he could be persuaded."

Tor shook his head. "The new teacher happens to be a woman. You might find it very hard to convince her that she's the father of your child."

Papik flared up. "You people can find more loopholes than a wolverine! Are there other white men here?"

"Only Knut," Tor said. "Who drinks firewater and the rest of the time is a policeman. But he isn't likely to take on a daughter either, especially if she's not his."

"A silly woman wants to try," Vivi said in despair.

Knut was the same policeman who had been present at the trial—a strong, tall redhead. They all trooped into his cabin, catching him in a dismally sober moment, and quite unwilling to become a father before acquiring a wife.

"A silly woman understands his reasons," Vivi requested Tor to tell him. "But please inform him that because women are scarce, many men marry a little girl and raise her to maturity."

Knut was shocked when Tor had translated this. "I'm not going to marry any little girl!" he thundered, reaching for the bottle.

Ootuniah had meanwhile grown hungry and restless, starting to cry and wetting the floor, and Papik's patience snapped. He sat the girl on the table and said:

"You take her. We leave."

"With the girl!" Tor growled, filling the doorway.

Papik turned to Vivi. "In Aage's town there is an orphans' home that takes children."

"And feeds them?"

"Yes. So much that everybody there would like to become an orphan. But one can get there only by the white man's boat. And they won't take you on board unless you have killed somebody."

"Remember, Papik," Tor said. "Knut will inform all the police, and if ever you can't say where the girl is, you will be punished for murder."

"We must try Ivaloo," Vivi told Papik.

"But by now Milak must have come back, or she has taken on a new husband. And it's a long trip."

"Ivaloo may still be waiting."

In a sudden frenzy, Papik flung his trundle hood to the floor, spat on it and trampled it.

"A man won't carry a baby! If Ootuniah can follow, good. If not, it's too bad. Whatever the police do or say." He turned to the white men: "Out of our way! Not one of your deserves to be Ootuniah's father!"

Never before had he been so angry at white men as with the present bunch. He was glad that they all invited him and his family to stay on for a while as their guests, so he could spurn their hospitality one by one, with a sniff of contempt. He stamped out of Knut's cabin, chin and chest thrust forward, ignoring Ootuniah. Vivi, already burdened with Ernenek on her back, lifted the girl in her arms and waddled after Papik.

Elated by the couple's decision to move on, the white men solicitously escorted them to the sled and helped them hitch the team. And when the sled started moving and they waved farewell, Papik did something he had never done before: he waved back.

Because for once he was glad to part company.

14

Marriage

The following spring, coming from Massacre Beach and still on their way to Pregnant Mountain, Papik and Vivi got the fright of their lives on seeing the ghost of Milak, Ivaloo's husband.

There he was, life-size and in bright daylight, frail-looking for a Man but as handsome as always, squatting over an ice hole together with another fisherman, and their woman nearby.

Her jerked around when his name was called, gazed at Papik and Vivi, his fine features a blank, and said in Milak's own voice.

"My name is Panipchuk."

"Are you not the husband of Ivaloo?" asked Papik.

The man denied it, wrinkling his nose, and jerked his head at the woman: "My wife."

Whereon Vivi tugged at Papik's sleeve and whispered: "Run!" And they ran, wide-eyed with terror.

For this could only mean that Milak had died and come back to life in exactly the same shape as before—there were even the two little scars on his lip from the challenge of a walrus bull—but inhabited by a different soul and name. A frightening discovery, like all unexplainable things, that prompted his in-laws to put a long distance between the apparition and themselves at once.

At the first stop while she tried to slumber, Vivi had an eerie feeling, like a frosty breeze caressing her neck. No sooner had she told Papik about it than he felt it too. So for some time thereafter neither of them dared to go to sleep unless the other kept watch.

But the matter disturbed them mostly for Ootuniah's sake. If Ivaloo had been informed of Milak's death, what would have stopped her from remarrying?

And a married Ivaloo would have no use for Ootuniah.

The trip to Pregnant Mountain, following a meandering course prescribed by wildlife and seasons, didn't take much over a year. Unless it was a little over two years. They were not sure. But they knew it was the peak of summer when they got there, for Pregnant Mountain was now an island, surrounded by tranquil waters, dark but pure, speckled with pans and bergs. A few umiaks were on the beach, reminders of the time when the settlement was a whaling base. Now they only served to ensure communication with the mainland to chase seal and walrus during the short period when the sea was navigable.

They found Ivaloo living in a new house of sod and whalebone, waiting with unchanged confidence for Milak to come back from his bear hunt. The entire village learned with relief that the Moon Man had had his vengeance by punishing Vivi with a girl, and nobody resented the couple's presence anymore.

"How about a husband?" Papik asked his sister, not naming Milak, since he was dead, for if the name hadn't found another body it would be hurt by being mentioned.

Ivaloo smiled broadly: "A silly woman was told that

Milak died and came back to life with a different soul
and name. Stupid gossip, of course."

"Of course," Papik nodded forcefully.

"We saw a man who looked exactly like him," Vivi
said before Papik could stop her. "And who turned
when we called him."

"But he said his name was Panipchuk," Papik said.

Ivaloo stared into the void, then smiled again. "There
are men who look like Milak."

"He had his voice and even the two scars," Vivi said.

"But not the same name and soul. Or else he would
have returned."

"While you wait for him, you could look after Ootuniah," Papik said. "That would help us keep Ernenek
safe."

"Yes, but Milak will surely want to move on and also
to beget a son as soon as he comes back," Ivaloo said.
"Then what about Ootuniah?"

"Keep her only until Milak returns," Vivi said. "Then
you may abandon her."

Ivaloo's eyes widened. "You talk as if Milak would
never come back! As if he were dead!"

"No, little one," Papik said. "Vivi just wants to see
our daughter safe, with you."

"It is impossible," Ivaloo said, hard. Then, reading
the despair on Vivi's face: "But it is not impossible that
somebody has a husband for Ootuniah. Willing to keep
her while she grows. It's not an unreasonable request,
with women so scarce."

"Of course," said Vivi. "If a man wants a wife of his
own, let him raise her!"

"Have a little patience. The man in question is out
hunting."

Tellerk was a Polar Eskimo whose main reason for
venturing south had been to find himself a new wife,

since the only fair-sized and unattached females he could find in his own regions were she-bears. During his first marriage he had proved himself a devoted husband, besides a real man.

That was why Ivaloo had suggested him.

Once he had left his first wife and their newborn son behind in a settlement. During his absence, the settlement was ravaged by an epidemic—one of the white men's diseases that was lethal only for the Eskimos. When he returned, whoever could move had fled, and the dogs and wolves were devouring the corpses and waiting for the last sick to die.

Through the shack's window, he saw his wife on her death-bed, nursing their baby. Though too afraid of the pestilence to enter, he didn't desert her, but kept hunting nearby, and threw food in to her through the window. It was only when he saw her dead, with the baby sucking frantically at her frozen breast, that he moved on.

"Someone will help you forget your dead wife," Ivaloo told him with one of her heartwarming smiles. "One's brother has arrived with his daughter. He might let you have her—if you promise to keep her."

Tellerk could hardly believe in his good fortune. "You have a brother? And he has a daughter?" He was a handsome devil, with one good eye and a lot of teeth —less burly but taller than Papik.

Ivaloo nodded. "A female daughter. Will you pledge to take her?"

"How old is she?"

"Oh, she's not old at all."

"Is she pretty?"

"If she isn't, you can return her."

Tellerk stamped about, to show that he couldn't be rushed into a hasty marriage, until Ivaloo told him:

"Mind you, Tellerk: you are the first man to receive

this offer, but not the last if you keep shifting on your feet."

So Tellerk gave his assent, and Ivaloo said that now the girl's father had to give his. She rapped her little drum, and Papik and Vivi, who had been hiding behind the house, came in, all smiles.

"This is Papik, one's brother," Ivaloo said.

"And this is the bride?" Tellerk looked delighted.

"No, no!" laughed Ivaloo. "That's the mother. What will you give them, to seal the agreement?"

"Where is the girl?"

"In our tent," said Papik. "Sleeping."

"Has she all her teeth?"

"Nearly all," Vivi said.

"So what will you give for her?" urged Ivaloo.

Tellerk was not one to miss out on a bargain. "A new shark's jaw that cuts the ice like blubber, and a long harpoon that took a man a whole winter to make. Hold everything! A man will get the dowry."

And he rushed out.

After the bridgroom had returned with the presents and the parents had accepted them, the agreement was binding on both parties, and nothing was left to do but to bring on the bride.

When Vivi reappeared with her little girl fast asleep in her arms, Tellerk's jaw dropped.

"This is Ootuniah!" Vivi beamed, holding up the child. "And she's all yours, to keep and hold!"

"To cherish and nourish!" exclaimed Papik.

"You make a marvelous couple!" said Ivaloo, moved.

"But . . . but . . ." Tellerk was beginning to find the strength to stutter—and to sink on the couch.

"Is she not pretty?" Vivi asked.

"She's not bad looking. But much too little!"

"She's not very big," Papik conceded, "but nice."

"And she will grow," Ivaloo promised. "Somebody told you she was not old. And you must know Kresuk. Don't you?"

"What about Kresuk?"

"He married his wife before she was born. Now they are very happy."

"Still, this isn't quite what a man expected," Tellerk said miserably.

Seeing him wavering, Vivi decided to intervene with force. "Why should we bring up a girl for a stranger? Pray tell."

Papik attacked his son-in-law from the other flank. "And let her go when she has muscles and learned to sew and scrape?"

"How selfish can you get?" Ivaloo added.

Tellerk wilted under the cross fire and looked so crestfallen and guilty that his in-laws finally took pity on him.

"You don't have to raise little Ootuniah all by yourself," Papik said. "You can travel with us. And Vivi will tend on her while we two go hunting together."

"You'll be my brother's guest," Ivaloo explained.

Tellerk perked up, and noticed that Vivi was smiling at him with teeth that looked almost new and eyes that shone brightly highlighting the blush on her cheeks.

And suddenly he felt much better about his marriage deal.

15

A Battle of Wits

Not wanting to embarrass Vivi and Tellerk with his presence while they made merry in his tent, Papik took the children to Ivaloo for a cup of tea and to thank her for ensuring Ootuniah's survival.

When Tellerk and Vivi joined him at Ivaloo's, they found the little house humming with conversation. One Gaba was visiting Ivaloo with his entire family. As a man of experience, he wanted to be on good terms with all angakoks, and he had made a detour just to pay his respects to this new one.

Gaba was a widely renowned husband and hunter. For years he had had three wives of his own, periodically replacing the one that had used up her teeth chewing his boots with one whose denture was intact. In at least one case he had drowned a new bride's parents before he could call her his own, but he had done it with so much tact that the police had never been able to prove it. Naturally every man envied him, but the women disapproved. If polyandry was perfectly acceptable to them, they regarded the reverse as shocking.

While a showdown between Papik and Tellerk was inevitable eventually, it was Gaba's presence that brought it on a little sooner.

Though they would never have admitted it, Papik and Tellerk felt inferior to Gaba because each of them had but a single wife, and one of these was furthermore rather small. Especially Tellerk resented the presence of that celebrity and his three women and one little son as a personal affront.

"Getting along with one wife is considered difficult enough," he told him on meeting him at Ivaloo's. "How do you manage to get along with three?"

"Easy," said Gaba, and spat in an elegant arch across the floor. "A husband has made a rule. When he talks, all his wives must shut up. When they talk, he doesn't listen."

Conceding Gaba's intellectual preeminence, Tellerk decided to challenge him on a manlier ground—hunting.

"Your good ladies," he chuckled, "look beautiful and elegant, but a bit starved in the waist."

This hurt.

"A man has arrived without provisions," Gaba said dryly. "But may he invite you all to a modest meal in one turn of the sun, after he has taken a nap?"

"A meal?" asked Tellerk. "Of what? If you have no provisions, and are now taking a nap—presumably in the company of three beautiful ladies."

Gaba ignored the following hilarity. When the laughter ebbed, he stopped picking his nose and said with deliberate casualness:

"Somebody will go hunting after his nap."

"We accept your invitation if you accept ours," Tellerk said.

Gaba got up and left in a huff, followed by his giggling covey.

"Somebody's good name is at stake," Tellerk told Papik. "We must bring home enough meat to put Gaba to shame."

Papik didn't answer. He was fuming because someone

else had been the life of the party. Tellerk had hogged the company's attention, had anticipated him in conversation every time, and was still holding the initiative. Moreover, Papik had noticed that Vivi had emerged more radiant than ever from the laughing session with her son-in-law, and now seemed to have eyes and ears for him only, applauding his most inane sallies with her ivory laughter.

"We shall go for walrus to Big Bear's Bay," Tellerk went on. "Ivaloo said that there's some safe ice there, and a walrus is just what we want to deflate that big bloated blubber bladder named Gaba."

Papik's patience snapped. "Who said we go to Big Bear's Bay?"

"This man said it," Tellerk replied haughtily. "Why?"

Papik swallowed hard. "Who decides the hunt?"

Tellerk feigned surprise. "Somebody just decided."

"This man decides!" Papik burst out.

"Not so."

For once no one laughed. This was plainly a crucial moment. His chest heaving, Papik rose, took the spear from the wall and pointed it at Tellerk's navel.

"Somebody has never taken orders," he said. "Let the spear decide."

Tellerk turned pale, and Ivaloo cried: "Wait, wait! You know that if one of you kills the other, he'll wish he hadn't. Even if the police don't get him, no man will ever again want his company. So let the drum decide and not the spear."

"It's the best way," Vivi said.

Drum songs are battles of wits and the only honorable way of solving disputes, welcome by all but the loser, for the entertainment they provide.

"A man accepts," Tellerk said.

"Because you're afraid of the spear!" cried Papik.

"Listen, Papik," said Ivaloo. "If you fight with the

spear, the loser will be dead, and the winner worse than dead. If you fight with the drum, the loser will merely be laughed at—and the winner applauded."

Papik couldn't admit that he would much rather be dead than laughed at. He merely said:

"A man is not afraid of the spear."

"Are you then afraid of a song?" Vivi asked slyly.

"A man is afraid of nothing!"

Whether Papik was the greatest hunter above the dog frontier could be a matter of dispute. But nobody, not even Papik himself, would have claimed that he was the Arctic's greatest bard. And poetic talent was required for the confrontation that was soon under way in Ivaloo's house, filled to the whalebone rafters by the happy audience that had flocked in as soon as word had spread.

Only Gaba and his wives had not been aroused from their slumber.

The cramped quarters were sultry with tightly packed bodies. The duellers' bare chests glistened, the sweat dropped from their faces upon the little drums that they rapped while they weaved and bobbed, singing out the verbal barbs designed to hurt the opponent's feelings by provoking the audience's hilarity, which was the final referee if none of the contestants conceded defeat. The crowd, seated on the floor, left little room for the two rivals, who remained planted on their feet in order not to stumble over the many legs, contorting only their torsos.

Tellerk's poetic gifts proved barely superior to Papik's. He launched into the fray with some stanzas that were good and some that were new, but the audience had heard the good ones before and didn't consider the new ones very good.

"Through his seals a man speaks against you, ayay-ay!" Tellerk wailed. "Through the many seals he has slain—the many more than you have slain, ayayay! And that give light to his igloo and happiness to his friends!"

"Ayayay!" came Papik's bleated reply. "Where are Tellerk's seals? A man only sees hopeful eyes and hungry stomachs—that he will fill, since Tellerk hasn't, ayayay!"

"Poor Papik is so thin that one could suspend his bow and harpoon on his ribs, ayayay!" Tellerk wailed in return, provoking laughter that would have been louder if Papik weren't bursting at the seams with brawn and fat.

"Hoh!" Papik snorted in contempt, swaying his dripping chest like a seal in love and rapping his drum. "Tellerk must muzzle his dogs and tie them to a stake, lest they devour him to survive, ayayay! Poor Tellerk! Poor dogs!"

Although most of the men and women present had witnessed more exciting drum duels, they were all determined to enjoy themselves and applauded the clumsiest attacks to fan the fires, but the performers' mimics and contortions remained more impressive than their lyrics and music. Soon both men were breaking the rules by cutting into the other's repartee, until the floor show consisted of two contestants rocking and chanting simultaneously, each one endeavoring to outshout his rival since he couldn't outwit him.

When Papik sang out, "Somebody is as clever as a fox and as strong as a musk ox—ayayay!" Tellerk banged his drum against Papik's and replied: "Somebody is, but not Papik—who is as strong as a fox and as clever as an ox, ayayay!" And he pushed his drum into Papik's face.

As the room became windy with laughter, Papik butted Tellerk in the forehead, who butted him in return, opening a gash on Papik's brow, and on his own as well. Papik replied by smashing his drum over Tellerk's head, then grabbed his stunned rival by the waist, raised him above his head, and took to smacking him against the low ceiling, shaking the whalebone rafters and showering everybody with sod.

"Is this the strength of a fox?" he thundered, blood trickling from his gashed brow. "Hoh? Hoh?"

"No, no!" whimpered Tellerk when his own face was sufficiently bloodied. "It's the strength of an ox!"

"And who is as clever as a fox?"

"You! You!"

"Shouldn't such a man lead the hunt?"

As the reply didn't come at once, Papik smacked him again, until Tellerk cried:

"You lead the hunt!"

"Now and always?"

"Yes, yes!"

Papik dropped his rival on the floor, but then helped him back to his feet and warmly shook hands with him, to show that he bore him no grudge—total reconciliation being a bounden duty after a duel of wits.

After the delighted visitors had left and Tellerk's hurt feelings had been salved with a cup of tea, Ivaloo asked her brother:

"Well then—what will you hunt?"

"Walrus in Big Bear's Bay," Papik said.

"That was Tellerk's proposal!"

"Yes. But he had to learn that the family head leads the hunt—and who the head is."

Papik was convinced that by settling the hunting question he had established all the premises for a family life of lasting harmony.

But soon he had to cope with a different problem.

16

The Widow

The walrus hunt was fruitful, and Gaba was so humiliated by the gifts of meat that Papik and Tellerk tried to heap on him, who had caught nothing, and on his wives, who hadn't caught anything either, that he left Pregnant Mountain fuming—and hungry to boot.

Papik's and Tellerk's success was chiefly due to Ivaloo, who had revealed to them the right spot, and they credited her uncanny powers rather than her knowledge of the neighborhood, as she did. Late summer, when the sea started freezing over but before the crust thickened, was a bad season for hunting. The birds had flown southward and wildlife had moved inland, except for some seal and walrus, but there was no way to set after them. The skin boats couldn't navigate lest they get crushed by the increasing flow of ice, and the sea crust that subsisted in a few narrow inlets wasn't thick enough to bear a man's weight.

With one exception.

Ivaloo, who by now had been living on that island longer than most, knew that in Big Bear's Bay the ice remained solid the year round, as the sun never touched it. If other villagers also knew about it they didn't inform Gaba, so even if he was a great hunter it was not during that brief stay at Pregnant Mountain that he was able to prove it.

Soon after his departure, Papik and Tellerk also left with their family, as the island was already overcrowded in relation to the available wildlife.

The hunt continued to absorb all their time and energies, but not in vain. Two hunters united could bag more game than separately. One of them would attract the quarry's attention while the other approached it from a different angle. Or one man could drive in a narrowing circle around a field of seals' breathing holes, blocking them off and leaving open only the one where his partner lay in wait. And they could put to use the long harpoon that had been part of Tellerk's dowry and required two men to operate.

In the summer they went inland after musk ox and caribou, consuming on the spot all the meat their bellies could hold, and sometimes more, and caching the rest in the hope of finding it again on some future occasion.

But meanwhile an unforeseen difficulty sprang up between Papik and Tellerk, concerning Vivi.

Papik treated Tellerk not merely as a son-in-law but also as a guest, whereas Tellerk acted as if he were a partner in Papik's own marriage. Papik discovered it once he came home and heard Vivi heatedly arguing with Tellerk.

The excitement of newness having worn off, Vivi had become again an average spouse, mindful of her husband and the moral values of her state. Of strait-laced upbringing, she respected the tradition that although a wife could be lent, sold, or given away, nothing may happen without the husband's knowledge and consent. This was a basic rule, known to all; but it could bear repeating, at least to some people.

And Tellerk was one of them.

"Why are you molesting Vivi?" Papik demanded with a scowl on coming in.

"Somebody wanted to talk to you about it," Tellerk said unflustered, though rubbing a swollen eye. "You should put in a word with Vivi. She wants your consent every time. But you are not always available."

"Vivi is right!"

"Why? A man doesn't use her up."

"It's not the usage, it's the principle!" Papik exploded. "If a man can't trust you in little things, how can he trust you in important ones?"

"Like what?" Tellerk sneered. As Papik couldn't think of a good instance, Tellerk went on: "So if you want to be mean, a man asks you now. Will you please leave? And allow him to exchange a bit of laughter with Vivi?"

Sarcasm was wasted on Papik, and he shouted: "No!"

"Miser!"

Papik flushed, for it was the first time he had been called that, and not without reason. However, a man couldn't back-track.

"Vivi is not your wife, for you to use as you please," he said. "Be patient, Ootuniah will grow. Meantime somebody will help you out, but when he says so, not when you say so."

"A man can do without your help!" And Tellerk rushed out to work off his anger on the dogs, while Vivi, red-faced for having caused a domestic quarrel, resumed her chores, avoiding Papik's eyes.

From then on it was plain that Tellerk wasn't going to abase himself by asking one more favor from Papik. And meanwhile also his rapport with Ootuniah wasn't such as might be expected between a married couple. There was no intimacy between them, and a complete lack of communication.

"Ootuniah won't play with me, she kicks me in the groin," he once complained to his mother-in-law.

"She's always been a bit shy of strangers," Vivi reassured him. "But she'll gain confidence with age, you'll see. All you need is patience."

Patience, however, was one of Tellerk's weakest traits. He grew surly and stopped all efforts to win his wife's affection. However, he made sure that she got plenty to eat, and frequently poked her naked belly to see whether she was gaining. But he always found that she was making very little progress.

He was wrong.

Both children were growing fast and fat on their fare of mother's milk enriched with live blood and fish and liver and seal oil and cuds of rotten meat that the little stomachs rejected at first, but eventually learned to retain.

Whereas little Ernenek revealed from the start a gay, frolicsome nature, Ootuniah was developing into a quieter, more reflective individual. The brass of her lank, already long hair, and her glacier-blue eyes, which were slightly crossed—not the least of her charms—lent her otherwise Asiatic face with high cheekbones the fascination of the unusual. The down that had adorned her arms and legs at birth had turned into stronger hairgrowth, unusual among the Men, who often remain hairless even in the crotch. Except with strangers, she was plucky and self-assured, perhaps because Ernenek looked up to her as a paragon and teacher, and she didn't want to let her little brother down.

The only complaints came from Tellerk, who apparently expected her to turn into a full-fledged woman overnight.

He became so sullen that Papik took pity on him and once, before leaving the igloo, led him again before Vivi with the traditional invitation: "Be one!" Tellerk tried to go on sulking, until Papik reminded him that no man could so offend a lady and keep his honest name. And Tellerk had to agree.

So harmony was restored.

Raising two small children at once proved just as hard as all the experienced voices had predicted, and it required the unflagging assistance of the guardian angels.

Outside its mother's hood, a small child is in constant danger. The ice is a treacherous element, with its countless pitfalls, crevasses, and channels. In spring it becomes even more dangerous. Nor is the summer a safer season, with all that water and the hunting forays inland. Then there is the constant threat from the famished pack. Dogs can be taught to leave children alone by dint of blows, and every child strong enough to lift a stick is taught to use it. But if a little one stumbles and falls, the pack pounces on it at once, pretending to believe that it is dog food thrown to them.

Vivi had other problems, too.

Her household chores had almost doubled with an additional man in the igloo, but there was no one to help her. She still had to nurse both children, and to skin and carve the kills of two hunters instead of one, sew and scrape and chew and mend everybody's boots and bearhides and birdskins and mittens, including her own.

And the strain was beginning to tell.

While the men snored, weary but satisfied, recovering their forces, she couldn't rest undisturbed for any length of time. One or the other child would wake her up—to tease her or demanding to play or to eat or to do the opposite. She complied as in a stupor, drugged with drowsiness, and yet pleased to be needed. It seemed indeed as if the brawn and gaiety that were deserting her were not lost, but passed on to her children. And she felt like making merry only with them.

"A woman doesn't care to laugh with Tellerk anymore," she once confided to Papik.

"Why? Is he disrespectful?"

"No, no. But a silly woman happens to be used to just one man, and doesn't like to double all the time."

"Small sacrifices are necessary, for our daughter's sake."

There was nothing Vivi could reply to that. But she no longer echoed the men's hilarity, and merely submitted to it, out of duty and therefore resentfully.

Until, without warning, death struck.

It occurred at the break of spring, more than two years after Ootuniah's marriage, when the family and the elements were emerging from the seasonal torpor.

The Air Spirits were whipping the Glacial Ocean and Sedna was churning the waters when Papik, peeking out of the tunnel, spotted a polar bear and went after it.

Their igloo was encased in the sea ice near the coast and the bear was headed for a promontory, where the danger of the frozen surface breaking during a storm was greater than elsewhere. But Papik couldn't resist the call of a bear hunt.

Karipari, running ahead with loud barks, seemed to feel likewise.

"Come back!" Tellerk yelled at Papik from the igloo, while the others crawled out into the open. Vivi waddled after Papik calling him back, the two children waddled after her out of habit, and the pack ran yapping after the leader.

Then the ice crust snapped, opening a long channel that engulfed the igloo together with Tellerk.

The whole family waddled back, hoping to rescue its latest member. If Tellerk could be fished out at once, he would be safe. His clothes, well sewn with seal's sinew that expanded in the wet, were watertight. But the channel had closed up again at once under the pressure of the surrounding crust, and the only sign of Tellerk was the handle of his knife emerging from the frosting, like a tomb marker.

By rights it was Papik who should have been engulfed for venturing into the danger zone. But the spirits don't always mete out retribution according to merit.

Thus little Ootuniah experienced the bitterness of widowhood long before tasting the sweetness of matrimony.

Papik and Vivi lost no time in exorcising Tellerk's shade.

They loudly lamented his end, magnifying his virtues while ignoring his defects. They scattered meat crumbs all around the spot of his departure and invited him to eat, in the hope that he might be mollified by their generosity and perhaps even help them get more in their next hunts. And then they drove off fast and far, stopping only to plant snares and pitfalls designed to trap the ghost if he should attempt to pursue them.

That a dead man should hate the living was as normal as that the lucky ones should proclaim their sorrow over his loss in the hope of ingratiating him. But Ootuniah's display of grief surprised her parents. Especially as it persisted after they had assured her that every safeguard against the shade had been taken. The little girl kept weeping hysterically, and when she was presented with the one comfort that had never failed before—her mother's bosom—she shrieked and belabored the offer with her little fists.

Her parents were nonplused. Ootuniah was very bright and even more precocious than most Men's children usually are; but after all, she was only some five or six years old, and until then had shown more attachment for one of Karipari's whelps than for any human member of the clan.

"Perhaps the spook has caught up with us and is hurting her," Vivi said.

Papik spat and stamped in anger. "That's all we needed! Most of our implements have gone down with the igloo and must be replaced—and now we also have to worry about a man's shade and a girl's tantrums!"

The riddle was solved shortly after they had built another snow shelter.

They were about to retire into their new abode when they spotted Ootuniah wandering off in the early morning gloom. As she ignored their calls, they went for her and dragged her back, struggling all the way.

"Let me be!" she cried. "Let me die!"

"Why should you die, little one?" Vivi asked, licking the tears from her daughter's eyes and wiping her nose with her own.

Ootuniah didn't answer, but eventually cried herself to sleep, whereafter her parents also dozed off. But suddenly Vivi woke up Papik, announcing:

"Ootuniah ran away! She wants to go to her death!"

"But why? She never cared for Tellerk."

"She always heard everybody extolling your mother for drowning herself when she became a widow, and maybe she feels she has to do the right thing, too. She is very impressionable."

"Ootuniah, impressionable?" Papik jeered. "Like a frozen bearhead!"

But meanwhile he had dressed. He handed little Ernenek to Vivi, who wouldn't sit out the outcome at home, and they followed Karipari's nose—a surer lead than the girl's little imprints on the windswept crust.

They stamped ahead against the gale, Papik holding

Karipari's line. Already Tellerk's absence was making itself felt. Little Ernenek weighed heavily on Vivi's back, but they couldn't have left him alone in the igloo, lest he wake up and find the way out.

Or the dogs the way in.

When they spotted Ootuniah crouched on the ice, they let Karipari run ahead, and waddled after the dog as fast as their high boots allowed.

Ootuniah was well, but not so the quarry she had harpooned in the breathing hole beneath her and which brimmed with foaming redness. Vivi was rewarded with a punch when she knelt down to Ootuniah's height and tried embracing her, for the girl was afraid of losing her catch, which was a big one. It took all of Papik's strength to pull it out of the water after widening the hole. It was a bearded seal, the kind whose hide makes the best dog harnesses.

Papik was aghast. "What have you done?" he cried.

Ootuniah took a defiant stance. "Somebody is a hunter! You can't let me die now!"

"But nobody, nobody wants you to die, little one!" Vivi said.

"A girl heard your chatter when you thought she slept. You kept her only because she had a husband," she pouted.

"We'll find you another husband, little one," Vivi said.

"Men don't want skinny little girls, but old fat ones like you!"

"You women!" Papik cried. "Blabbering at a moment like this!" He was beating his head so hard that it sounded hollow. "Our daughter has offended sealdom, and now all the sea creatures will avoid us!"

"Why?" Vivi asked, terrified. "Does the taboo apply to children, too?"

"The affront is worse—being killed not only by a female, but by a little one!"

"Ootuniah didn't know! What can we do?"

"Only one thing," Papik said dejectedly. "Try to out-run the soul of this seal—and keep running."

17

The Boys

They did whatever was in their power to placate seal-dom. First of all Papik looked for some sweet ice. Ice-bergs are drinkable, for they are the children of glaciers, born on land, from snow that eventually turns to ice. The bergs Papik saw trapped in the sea crust were too far away, but even the sea ice loses its salinity and becomes potable when it remains long frozen, as the brine held by the crystals drains off in time. Papik didn't know this, though he knew how to recognize sweet patches by their dark transparency, in contrast with salt ice, which is white and opaque.

He melted a mouthful of sweet ice and spewed it into the dead seal's gullet, for animals that live in salt water are bound to be always thirsty. Then every member of the family ate morsels of the heart and liver, in the hope that the seal, if it came back to life bent on vengeance, would respect people of whom it had become part. As a rule, tasting a victim's vital organs to conciliate the shade was a ritual performed only with human bodies, after a murder, but the gravity of the offense advised Papik to leave nothing untried. Next, instead of returning to the sea only a few bones of the victim, as Sedna prescribed, he dropped the entire carcass into the water, hoping to mollify the old Queen by such a grand gesture.

Then he readied the sled and kept it skidding over the ocean until the team broke down.

For many turns of the sun thereafter, the family lived in the dread fear that word of Ootuniah's crime might spread among the sea creatures. The little girl herself felt increasingly guilty about her irresponsible deed and started brooding over her parents' disapproval, although in her presence they professed to have forgotten it.

In her childish ignorance of taboos, Ootuniah thought that if she made the spirits believe she was a boy, the family might go scot-free. How could one tell females from males? Females spoke low, sewed, scraped, carved, sat silently in the background while the men discussed important matters; and females groomed their hair, raising it to a turret like her mother or braiding it like her aunt or letting it softly enfold the face. Men spoke harshly, thrusting chin and stomach forward, and allowed their hair to become matted from neglect and to fall where it would, at the most slashing it off with a knife over their eyes when it interfered too much with their vision.

Any other differences were not apparent, as men and women wore identical clothes, and Ootuniah hoped that the spirits had no private way of telling them apart.

She had recently started learning how to sew and scrape, but after her slaying of the seal she refused to touch another needle or do any kind of housework again. She stopped combing her hair, acted rough, spoke harshly, thrust her little chin and stomach out, and insisted on accompanying her father on all his hunting forays.

She built herself a spear and learned to thrust it so deftly that Papik made her also a little bow of bone and sinew, with which she could shoot down birds. But it was only when the sealing season started and **Papik** met with no unusual difficulties, and even Ootuniah bagged another one, that he began believing in the effectiveness of the girl's stratagem.

And that the family wasn't doomed.

The next year, traveling along Beartongue Channel in search of driftwood and mayhap some other bachelor on whom to palm off the little girl, they came across a sled of Netchillik who relayed a communication from Ivaloo.

The Netchillik ride around the top of the world on their sleds of frozen meat or fish even more restlessly than the Polar Men, to whom they actually feel superior. So whenever Papik encountered some, he found it very hard not to burst out laughing in their faces.

"Are you really Papik? The brother of Ivaloo, the angakok?" inquired the Netchillik man.

"It is not impossible," said Papik. "Why?"

"Somebody has a message for Ivaloo's little niece. But one only sees two boys."

Papik's children were standing at his side, both in their bearskin trousers, barechested, sunburnt, wild-maned, clutching their blood-crusted spears. Ootuniah's hair and eyes were especially bright in summer, by contrast with her coppery skin; Ernenek's hair was blue-black like his parents', and his eyes as smoky as theirs.

Papik swept the landscape, making sure there was no sea animal around that could overhear.

"These are our children," he said then. "The one that looks rougher than the other is the girl."

"The blonde?" The Netchillik snickered and scratched his head. "Is she a white man's offspring?"

"It is not impossible," Papik snickered back, while the Netchillik woman and Vivi exchanged smirks and giggles. "What is the message?"

"Ivaloo wants the girl at Pregnant Mountain at once."

"Why?"

"Who knows? We have it from others."

They surmised that Ivaloo had heard of Tellerk's passing and had a new bridegroom ready for the little girl. Or else that Milak had returned and Ivaloo had prevailed upon him to adopt Ootuniah until they had a son of their own to worry about. In either case it was necessary to hurry.

But it was also necessary to eat.

Going for game, skinning and eating the kills and caching the surplus, waiting for the sea to freeze and then for the darkest night to pass, a good year went by before they were once more rubbing noses with Papik's sister at Pregnant Mountain.

Ivaloo's smile appeared a little broader, her gaze even more lost than before.

She said that Milak had returned, but only in her dreams. So it was not impossible that he was dead. But she didn't wish to go away with another man, for Milak had promised to return to her regularly in her sleep, and if she left he might be unable to find her again. So for the time being, she could look after Ootuniah. Secure in her position as an angakok of growing renown, she could take the little girl off her brother's back.

When Ootuniah heard that her parents would leave without her, she burst into tears, which only Papik's stern reminder that Men don't cry brought to a stop. Grown as close to her family as a limb to a body, she couldn't conceive of losing them, nor of a different life —renouncing the sled runs over the Glacial Ocean, the hasty building of shelters in the stifling blizzard, the hunting forays close to her father's boots, the setting of trap lines, the tilts with bears, the taming of the team, the fashioning of implements in the cozy igloo, to the howls of the Air Spirits and the growls of the Sea

Queen. And the delicious cuds her mother sometimes still·fed her mouth-to-mouth as a special treat; not to mention the sweetness of her nipple, while little Ernenek sucked and slurped on the other one, and his black eyes were anchored in his sisters, or his thumb playfully poked her cheek.

"When winter comes," Ivaloo tried consoling Ootuniah, "we'll build ourselves an igloo on the bay ice."

Big deal. Just she and the old aunt.

"Meanwhile you will have playmates," Ivaloo went on enticingly. "They'll teach you how to turn somersaults with a kayak without getting water into your clothes, to collect eggs on the cliffs, and to compete in bird catching contests."

Bird catching contests!

She went anyway up the bird cliffs, with two other children armed with nets attached to long poles, on an auklet capturing spree, but just to be sociable—a considerable effort for one who didn't easily take to strangers. Little Ernenek had wanted to join, but his mother wouldn't let him out of her sight. The family needed the son.

When the two village children had netted their first auklet, they strung it through the beak, suspended it between two sticks, and lay in wait for the others that came lured by the flappings of the captive. Each new catch was added to the preceding ones, until the spot was alive with flapping auklets, which attracted ever more quarries.

At the end the children had caught so many birds that carrying them home was a problem.

To Ootuniah, her companions' pride and joy over catching a mess of auklets was laughable, but she said nothing. She considered it beneath her to tell them of her secret ambition—of spearing a full-grown polar bear all on her own, while the adults slept—which would have been quite a feat for a girl who was about seven years old, give or take a year. She had wanted to make her father proud of her, so that he would acknowledge that she was a real hunter. But that was past now.

She hadn't the slightest ambition to impress fishers and bird catchers.

The adults in Ivaloo's house were sleeping; Ootuniah couldn't. She was afraid of dropping off to sleep lest she wake up to find her family gone; without farewells, of course, as the parting would be painful for them, too.

She looked around in the gloomy little house. Her father was snoring like a walrus. Her mother tossed fitfully. Ivaloo slept placidly, smiling in her mild insanity, probably dreaming of Milak. And little Ernenek?

Ernenek was missing.

Ootuniah didn't awaken her parents, always fearing that then they might leave; after finding Ernenek, of course. She took her spear and headed for the bird cliffs, with Karipari. Ernenek had been very unhappy when his parents hadn't allowed him to go birding with his sister.

And there she spotted him, on a cliff over a shallow pool of water that a frolicking walrus family was keeping open in the ice.

He had reached the first ledge several feet high and was crawling precariously toward a line of auklets perched there. Ootuniah called out to him not to move, but he merely smiled at her and crawled on. Abandoning her spear and Karipari, she scrambled up the cliff.

The auklets let Ernenek come almost within reach, then fluttered off, and as the boy grabbed for them he dropped and tumbled into the walrus pool.

Ootuniah hastened back down to regain her spear, flaying her hands on the rocks, then waded into the pool where Ernenek was splashing about, breathless with terror, as yet unable to cry.

The puzzled walruses had interrupted their games. On seeing Ootuniah, a massive bull bestirred itself to charge her.

The challenge of a bull heavier than ten seals would have been dangerous even for Papik. Ootuniah managed to pull Ernenek out, then ran with him along the gravel beach to safety. The walrus, fish in the water, couldn't move much faster than fish on land.

The two children stopped, panting and tittering. Both had got wet, for they weren't wearing their traveling clothes, and Ootuniah raced Ernenek up a slope to warm him, followed by joyful Karipari.

Up on a platform on top of the slope, they lit upon two bears with a pair of almost grown-up cubs. Like the Polar Men, the polar bears sometimes venture inland in the summer to satisfy their natural curiosity by exploring unknown territory.

Just as surely as she knew that some day she was going to kill a bear, Ootuniah knew that this was not the day. She didn't want to leave her brother's hand. And he couldn't run fast enough. Nor was he aware of the danger. He was snickering, pointing his little spear at the bears.

As the largest one shambled closer, Karipari snarled into action, lunging at the bear's throat with its broken fangs. The bear crushed the dog in its mighty embrace and started gnawing into its neck. Ootuniah's knees wobbled. Without her brother, she would have rushed to Karipari's aid, trying to pierce a rear tendon of the bear or the thin skin under its chin. Now she couldn't even retreat. The other bears had circled her.

The big bear dropped the dying Karipari and headed for the two children.

Never before had Ootuniah so regretted that she was still so little. She knew that bears avoided men unless very hungry, and these didn't seem hungry. But neither did they seem to regard the children as human beings, owing to their size perhaps. They were moving in.

She tried to think of her father's teachings: "Don't shout when wild animals approach. Speak to them, warm and low, like a mother. Puzzle them."

She hoisted Ernenek upon her shoulders and told him to raise his arms. He tittered with glee. With Ernenek on her shoulders, Ootuniah cut as tall a figure as ever faced a polar bear. And she addressed the attacker in a low, soft voice.

"Little bear, you may be the son of the one that killed grandfather Ernenek." Not the words mattered but the tone. "Your liver is very tasty when warm, but your meat is better frozen, nobody knows why. Only your tongue and hams always taste good. But you may keep them, and also your big heart, little bear."

Ernenek threw his little spear then.

It bounced harmlessly off the thick bearhide. Frightened, the animal jumped back. By now the others also seemed perplexed by the sounds and antics of the towering, many-limbed figure, and Ootuniah started a cautious retreat to safer ground. The bears followed her for a little stretch and then returned to inspect Karipari's carcass.

When they were out of sight, Ootuniah sat down with a snort of relief.

"Never, never go away again!" she told her brother.

"Somebody wants to kill a bear," he snickered. "And a wolf."

"When your time comes. Not now."

"Now!" Ernenek was pointing. "Woof! Woof! The time of the wolf is now!"

So it was: a pack of wolves had been trailing the two children.

When the parents, escorted by the entire team, located them half a turn of the sun later, the children had taken shelter in a small-mouthed cave, blocking the opening. Little Ernenek was joyfully throwing rocks at the beseigers. Ootuniah was beating off with her spear every wolf nose that appeared in the opening.

While Papik and the dogs battled the wolves, Vivi embraced her children.

"A mother will never let you go, little one," she told Ootuniah. "You are a hunter now! We couldn't do without you."

But whereas Ernenek had allowed himself to be sniffed at and nose-rubbed, Ootuniah, still resentful, rammed an elbow into her mother's belly.

18

The Men

The years went by and Papik's family went on living;
life being mainly a matter of surviving.

The parents grew old as precociously as the children
grew up, carved by an inflexible habitat; like the scattering of other Men who, secure in their icy fastness, still
live in the ways of their ancestors—weathering the polar
nights in blisters of snow heated only by the warmth of
human bodies; practicing infanticide, suicide, euthana-
sia, incest, superstition, the community of goods and the
therapy of laughter, tempered by occasional manslaughter and cannibalism.

And loving life without fearing death.

It was as if Papik's family had two sons. Ever since
Ernenek had been strong enough to hold his father's
heavy knife, he had been allowed to handle it. If he cut
himself, it was a good lesson. Loving a son included
awakening him to the hazards of life. Soon the boy
learned to greet the sight of his own blood with a snicker, since he wasn't allowed to cry. He started bringing in
skinfuls of birds shot down with arrows; and before long
his first seal, too.

Ootuniah meanwhile developed into a valid hunter

long before little Ernenek caught up with her. But one stroke of luck that helped her bag her first bear caused her also to rely excessively on her guardian angel, until another event taught her that angels can't always be trusted.

A Man in need of food sometimes tries to ferret out bears in their winter dugouts with the help of a dog. Love spells the downfall of many a good bear, inducing it to dig an igloo in the ice for the cubs and to watch over the female during her confinement. The bears' igloo, after which the Men have patterned theirs, is provided with a winding tunnel that admits air but no wind.

Dogs are childish and impetuous, far less prudent and crafty than the animals of the ice, and they couldn't live in the Arctic without the help of man. In its eagerness, the dog that scents a bear may lead its master on top of the dugout, causing the roof to cave in. Papik had known one Nessark who had ended in this way. So as soon as Ootuniah was strong enough to hold on to a leash he started sending her ahead with the dog, for a bear's igloo is less likely to collapse under a child's weight. And while the girl stood on top of the dugout with the foaming, burrowing, snarling dog, Papik would locate the tunnel and lunge in with his spear in one hand and his knife in the other.

But meanwhile Ootuniah was growing. How much, the family discovered the time she broke into a dugout, tumbling with her dog upon a bear couple.

When Papik rushed to her aid, Ootuniah had nailed the male to the icewall through the gaping jaws, while the she-bear was grappling with the dog. Ootuniah couldn't get her spear-head back out of the ice and had pulled her flint knive. But no half-grown girl can overcome a ton of bear with a knife unless she gets him to fall in love with her first, and Ootuniah was saved only by her father's prompt arrival. After that, Papik resorted to little Ernenek for seeking out bears in their winter quarters, to the boy's immense delight.

But meanwhile Ootuniah considered herself second to no one, and Papik had to caution her constantly.

In all this, Vivi remained burdened with the entire housework, and any attempt to remind her daughter of the feminine duties met with rebuffs.

"If you can't sew, you'll never find a husband," Vivi once menaced.

"A hunter needs no husband!" Ootuniah answered back.

"But you need clothes. What will you do about them?"

"She could take a wife," was little Ernenek's suggestion, which almost brought the house down.

"There won't always be a mother to sew for you," Vivi went on.

Suddenly alarmed, Ootuniah took refuge in Vivi's lap. "Why? You won't leave me!"

"Sooner or later everybody leaves, little one."

"But not you! You're always at home."

"Everybody leaves." Vivi clasped her closer and rocked her as when she was small. "But don't let it worry you. You'll leave your mother before she leaves you."

"A girl will never leave you!"

"You will, little one. When you discover that you want a husband more than a father and mother. And then you'll wish that you knew how to sew."

"Never!"

For all her daughter's attachment, Vivi missed not only her help in the house but all too often the comfort of her company as well. Since both children went hunting far afield with their father, they couldn't suckle on their mother's breast regularly anymore, and to keep lactation going and ensure her barrenness Vivi had to put the whelps on her black nipples, which were prodigiously elongated and creviced from the relentless usage.

When Ootuniah returned from her forays with the men, she was as tired as they were. If bad weather kept them indoors, she slept or worked on the weapons and gear, like her father and brother. She only spoke of hunting, never housework. The rare times they came across other sleds or igloos and she succeeded in overcoming her shyness of strangers, she conversed with the men, not the women, with whom she shared no interests. And as she wanted to pass for a boy, she endeavored to look and act rougher than any one of them. She spoke harshly and allowed her long, lank hair to get matted and tangled with soot and blubber, like her father, instead of washing it in urine and combing it with the long fish spine, like her mother, who was always beautifully groomed, even when she had nobody to impress but her own husband.

Which was usually the year round.

They had never heard of Aage again, nor met any other member of his tribe or someone who had known him or had been to that remote fishing town. But they kept track of their fellow Men's destinies through their encounters with other sleds or igloos. The news was never recent and seldom reliable, but its rarity made it always interesting, and sometimes sensational—like one item concerning Ivaloo.

According to several voices, Papik's sister had borne a child of her own, but nobody could tell them whether Milak had found his way back or Ivaloo had replaced him.

Another juicy item concerned Gaba, the triple-domed lady killer, who had come to grief in an icebreak. Gossip had it that before tumbling into the water he had been murdered—by the five bachelors who had then undertaken to console his three widows.

Old Ammahladok and his wife Egurk hadn't been seen again, and the igloo where Papik and Vivi had left them years ago had probably turned into their tomb, melting with the icescape.

Nothing is supposed to last, not even graves, but there is a ghost of a chance that those embedded in the polar frosting will.

Papik's family discovered one such icy grave while digging for an elusive cache once when they were out of food. They never found the cache, but they uncovered an igloo built and equipped exactly like theirs, except that the faces of the occupants, a couple with a small boy, all perfectly preserved, seemed made of bluish, polished leather, and the familiar implements included a puzzling item—a sharply curved ivory tusk, as big as a man, from some unknown animal. Although cumbersome, Papik carried it along on his sled, hoping it might turn out to be a powerful good-luck charm.

But the hunting continued being so poor that he concluded the tusk was more likely an instrument of bad luck, and he got rid of it.

When little Ernenek was no longer so very little, entering puberty and approaching Ootuniah's stature, he started resenting his sister's authority and patronizing ways. He had discovered that males and females had separate, clearly defined tasks: that other girls didn't hunt and no other boy would follow his sister's lead.

Once upon a time Ootuniah had been twice as big and thrice as smart as he—a valid ground for looking up to her. But after she had stopped growing and he was quickly catching up to her, and discovering that she wasn't nearly as tall as she had seemed at one time, he saw no reason why her domination should continue. His rebellion sparked a hot strife between them, as they vied with each other for their father's consideration.

Papik paid for this rivalry with three fingers of his left hand.

Flouting the rule never to venture far afield by herself, Ootuniah had left the sleeping family to pursue a bear she had spotted prowling in the gloom of fall. The wily animal lured her up a glacier that was safe for its spiked and bristly pads but slippery for sealskin boots. Trying for a shortcut that would bring her face to face with her quarry, Ootuniah leaped a narrow crevice, skidded, and tumbled in.

Glacier crevices are beautiful to look at but ugly to drop into—dark blue wedges, like slashes from a gigantic axe, narrowing toward the bottom and solidly entrapping their catches.

By the time Papik had located Ootuniah with the help of his best scent dog, she was barely conscious and half frozen. And they found her mainly because the bear had reversed the roles, turning from quarry into hunter. It was swaying its head over the crevice, trying to devise a way to get at the catch.

Papik had to rip his jacket into strips and knot them to a line and had to call upon all his strength and fishing skill to retrieve the girl. Whereon he replaced her frozen mittens with his own and loaded her on his shoulders, leaving his hands exposed.

In the igloo the family and the whelps piled upon the girl to infuse their warmth into her, and one dog was slaughtered so that Ootuniah might plunge her hands into the steaming bowels. At the same time her parents tried to warm her from within by arousing her hilarity, which could be almost as effective as anger. She finally burst into a saving laughter when Papik told her of the white explorer whose frozen face was rubbed with such force by his companions, who believed in harsh treat-

ment to reactivate circulation, that his nose broke off
like an icicle. Still, it took several sleeps before Ootuniah was quite herself again.

But not Papik. Depleted, he had dropped off to sleep,
with his icy feet against Vivi's stomach but oblivious of
the numbness in his hands. When he woke up, it was too
late. Three fingers couldn't be revived. In time, they
turned blue and gangrene set in. When it became necessary to amputate them, he asked Ootuniah to attend to
it, as a punishment and lesson. And she obeyed without
a word, barely wincing as she slammed down the axe.

To prove that she was a real Man.

Long before the fever and pain had subsided, Papik
tried to laugh off the little mishap, saying it was better
to lose three fingers than two feet. After all, he could
stilll count up to seventeen. But some of his gaiety had
deserted him together with those fingers. The incident
had reminded him that he was not indestructible, and
made him notice other handicaps of advancing age. He
was less prompt in getting up after a fall. His children
turned out to be right more often when they asserted
that what he had mistaken for an ice block was a bear
or what had appeared as a seal to his eyes was merely
driftwood. And along with his own shortcomings, he
also noticed that Vivi's tail end had broadened and her
beautiful teeth had turned shorter and darker by dint of
chewing hides. But there was one compensation to aging
—seeing one's children grow up.

Ernenek looked more and more like his namesake
grandfather. And when he had grown as tall and much
sturdier than his sister, he recovered the true Men's
gaiety that he had mislaid for awhile.

As for Ootuniah, her body underwent early the expected changes. Her formerly boyish chest sprouted
breasts that seemed to defy the law of gravity, with the

complicity of vigorous pectorals. The protruding belly, hallmark of every real Man, shrank together with her appetite, whereas the flat buttocks developed bulges that not even the bearhide pants could entirely conceal. And the dark hairgrowth that once shaded her limbs disappeared, concentrating elsewhere.

Vivi discovered all this overnight, in the course of the body scraping to which she submitted her family once each spring, after everyone had stripped for the first touch of the sun.

New, disturbing instincts had started early to stir the girl's blood, rendering her restless and alarming her the more because they eluded her comprehension. She didn't confide in anyone and grew increasingly taciturn. But Vivi didn't have to be told. In vain did she exaggerate her own failing eyesight and stiffening fingers in the hope of enlisting her daughter's help and to start training her as a housewife.

Ootuniah continued to act as if touching a needle or a garment scraper were taboo.

Although Pregnant Mountain was off their regular circuit, Vivi asked to revisit Ivaloo when they hadn't seen her for several years; first because she wanted Ootuniah to meet people, and then to satisfy her own curiosity about the several children Ivaloo was rumored to have, though there was still no information about a husband.

This mystery alone certainly justified the longest detour.

They reached Pregnant Mountain in the dark of night, when the bay ice was spangled with the salmon-hued glow of all the little winter igloos. In one of them they found Ivaloo, looking her old placid self, a bit heavier around the middle and the cheeks, and warmed by no less than five children—three girls and two boys, not to mention a new one she was about to spawn—to whose upkeep the whole community was contributing, wanting to keep their angakok happy. Two more children of hers had died—one from drowning, another lacerated by dogs. In all this, no trace of a husband. But certainly Ivaloo could explain.

"Did you adopt them or inadvertently look at the full moon?" inquired Papik, who had not forgotten that exposure to moonlight might induce pregnancy, as any number of husbandless women could confirm.

"It is not impossible," Ivaloo said with her vacant smile. "But a woman is sure that it wasn't only the moonlight. It's Milak who keeps coming in my dreams, as he had promised. But it must remain a secret."

"Why?"

"It could start new rumors of interference from on High, and bring a woman in trouble again."

Papik and Vivi promised to guard her secret, and were glad to see her rejoicing in her growing rookery of boys and girls.

Of course, men had meanwhile been coming from all over, and kept coming, proposing to take Ivaloo for a wife and let the children shift for themselves. But she had no intention of abandoning them, and kept turning down their flattering offers.

"What about Ootuniah?" she inquired. "Every bachelor would be glad to take her, now that she is ready."

Vivi, who had relished the conversation up to that point, frowned and said:

"She isn't. She can't sew and refuses to learn. A mother hopes she will meet a man who will change her."

"A girl wants no husband to order her around!" Ootuniah said.

"A time will come when you'll want children, little one," Ivaloo told her. "You'll see."

"Never! Children are noisy and messy and a bother."

"There are things you can't understand before you fully grow up. And then you'll wish you had lent an ear to those who know."

Ootuniah lifted her chin in contempt and wrinkled her nose.

But less than a year later her aunt's prophecy came true in the most unexpected manner, catching the whole family napping.

And shattering the routine of their lives with a crash and a fracture.

19

Where People Undress

The next best thing to fighting a blizzard on top of the
world is to lie safely in a cozy igloo, pitying the hapless
devils outside.

While traveling at winter's end over the Glacial
Ocean, during the period when a brief luminescence
heralds the coming of the sun at each turn, they had
spotted mysterious lights in the coastal gloom. These led
to a small group of buildings—angular edifices of cement and cabins of corrugated iron, which could only
mean the presence of white men, but clearly belonging
to a different tribe from Aage's, who built peaked cabins and rambling houses of frame on stilts. They had
never encountered white men that far north before.
There were also a few native huts, partly dug in the
ground, cowering under the elements. And piles of
packing cases and oil drums.

When the family reached the spot, all was dark and
nothing stirred, as if everyone were asleep.

As they were tired and not presentable, they dropped
their sled anchor, erected a snow shelter, hung up their
soggy garments, and went to rest.

They were sleeping in one another's warmth and faint

daylight was fingering through the snow wall when Vivi woke up to a barking concert of the team, conducted by Noonah, their latest lead dog. She was nonplused on hearing a dull rumble and feeling the ground shake, for she was sure that they had not erected the igloo on the sea ice but on the coast, near the houses. She was pinching the thick skin of Papik's stomach to wake him up when their shelter crumbled and an iron monster thundered across, filling the air with stench and leaving the little dome a shambles, human limbs stirring numbly in the snow.

The monster was a bulldozer.

Since it was longer than the whole igloo and the floor of the shelter was dug into the surface of the ground, the caterpillar tracks passed harmlessly over the lying bodies —except Papik. He had jumped to his feet too quickly, and the machine brushed his leg and hip, cracking bones and spilling blood.

When he discovered that the white man who drove the monster had not harmed him intentionally but was flustered and eager to make amends, Papik apologized for having been in the way and tried to smile while grimacing in pain—which took some doing. He was carried into a small iron cabin that was equipped as an infirmary, with magic jars and bottles lurking in a cabinet, awe-inspiring instruments of gleaming metal hanging from the bare iron walls, and a white angakok and one of those female assistants trained to puncture the helpless. This nurse also was an Eskimo.

The hut had but one room and the room had four beds and the beds only one occupant—Papik.

He became uneasy when he saw once more what the white men could achieve with their magic paraphernalia —like removing the pain of his shattered bones with a single puncture. That really scared him. Anybody who could do that was obviously allied with the devil.

With whom the Men, to their great chagrin, had never been able to establish a solid alliance.

Emerging with spinning head from the deep slumber into which he had sunk after the injection, Papik received another shock on seeing the white angakok and the nurse hovering over him with masks of cloth that left only their eyes exposed. Then he remembered having seen similar masks at the hospital in Aage's town, and he felt reassured: they must serve to scare away the evil spirits that cause pain.

His injured thigh and leg were encased in plaster and under traction, held aloft by a rope suspended from the ceiling—a white men's exorcism against broken bones.

"You are lucky that the white men are here," the nurse giggled at him. "Without them, who would repair your bones?"

Papik was too weak to answer.

There was an iron stove that burned some malodorous fuel and kept the room much too warm, but the white angakok had worn his fur jacket also while working on his patient. When he removed his mask he turned out to be wearing fur even on his face, in the form of a trim blond beard; whereas Papik was awash in sweat, although he wore nothing but his plaster cast.

For relief he looked at the frosted windowpanes.

The doctor had left and the absent sun had done half a turn before Papik found the strength to ask Igah, the nurse, about his wife and children. They had remained outside on the sled, over which they had pitched their tent against the raw weather, and were waiting patiently.

Igah called them in.

Noonah, their dog, bounded at once on its master to lick the blubber from his face while the other members of the family swept into the room with expectant grins, stamping the snow from their boots and sniffing the unfamiliar scents. The sight of Papik lying naked in his sweat, his plastered leg roped to the ceiling, almost broke them up. Then they took off their hides and hung them on the lamp and all around the room, to drip and dry lest they rot.

While Ernenek probed and knocked Papik's cast, Ootuniah presented the bowlful of rotted meats, now frozen, brought along to speed her father's recovery. But the injection had removed his appetite together with the pain, and his delighted relatives proceeded to consume the delicacy themselves, throwing the bones to Noonah.

From the moment they had entered, nurse Igah had made a nuisance of herself, objecting to everything they did and trying to kick the dog out. This was surprising, since Igah was an Eskimo and should have known manners. They hadn't discovered yet that she was addicted to alcohol, which affected her moods. When Papik had woken up from the operation, she had been high on cough syrup and in a gay frame of mind. Now she was sober and therefore querulous.

The members of Papik's family had been taught to endure practically anything when in somebody else's igloo, especially a white man's, and they showed their disapproval of Igah's behavior merely by ignoring her; a strategy that proved effective.

When the nurse finally stamped out, muttering darkly, the visitors groaned with relief and let their hair down. They flung the windows open to let cold air in and hot odors out. Ernenek laid himself down at his father's side and at the same time Vivi tried the other side. As the cot wasn't built for three, and barely for one, it collapsed with a bang, leaving Papik dangling by his leg. Everybody howled. Papik, from pain.

But soon he also joined in the general hilarity.

It would have been a very successful visit if nurse

Igah hadn't spoiled it, coming back with the doctor.

The children, who had seen their first real white men that day, while waiting on the sled, and then not so close, gazed at him in awe.

They were not the only ones to display surprise. The doctor looked in amazement around the room—the garments hung to dry, the smashed cot, the scattered bones, the dog who had never smelled a white man before and who was barking at him angrily—then addressed his nurse in angry tones. It was fortunate that the family didn't understand him. But once more Igah couldn't leave a good thing alone and played interpreter.

"You are messy!" she scolded the consternated visitors. "And you smell!"

As soon as she had recovered from her surprise, Vivi snapped back: "So do you! But you smell bad! Peuh!" And she spat on Igah's boots.

The white angakok spoke fluently three words of the Men's language—"Boy," "Woman," and "Out"—and he used them all, underscoring them with gestures. Vivi regretted at once her rash reply, and it dawned on her that they might be in trouble.

"Let us take Father out of here," she whispered to her children. "These people are dangerous."

"You can't take him before he can walk," Igah said.

"We'll give you all the food we have on our sled and then go hunting for you."

Igah couldn't help but smile. "You don't understand. He's in no danger here. The white men feel responsible for his injury, and they can't let him go before making him well again."

"You mean, like a taboo?"

"About."

Vivi dropped her shoulders. She knew when she was licked.

"Out, woman!" the doctor repeated, pointing at the door. "Out, boys!"

Ootuniah gaped at him, scratching her head. "Boys?" She wrinkled her nose and declared: "Somebody is a girl, not a boy."

"What did he say?" asked the doctor.

"It seems we have a girl here," Igah said.

The doctor stared incredulously at Ootuniah, asked his nurse to repeat, then burst into uproarious laughter —and from the gleam of his teeth and pinkness of his gums, Ootuniah could tell that he was very young. He had an amusing face, with a funny, tilted nose that moved when he laughed.

Ootuniah hadn't expected such gaiety from a white man. And at first she resented his laughter, for it was plainly over her. But it sounded so warm and free of malice that she finally joined in, tentatively. Unless there was another reason. This was the season when the seals, experiencing the stirrings of spring, were preparing to defy danger and venture out of the waters, in quest of a mate.

And it was Ootuniah's first springtime since she had grown to womanhood.

20

Snow White

When the sky cleared and they grated the ice from the windowpanes, Papik and his family got a closer look at something that until then they had seen rarely and only from very far away: airplanes. Those they had seen before, streaking the Arctic sky at great height and bridging continents, had seemed tiny. The ones they saw now were much smaller but looked large, for they came close to the window before they bounced to a landing with their ski-pontoons on the coastal strip the bulldozer had thoughtfully leveled out for them.

Most of the foreigners here seemed to be angakoks, arriving out of the sky and leaving again by air in an infernal noise. The camp, set up by a foreign enterprise a few seasons earlier and named Snow White, was girding for a brief summer of intense activity. Not only the foreigners who lived in the cement and iron dwellings but also the Eskimos who worked for them or gravitated around the Company Center were more than Papik could count on his fingers and toes—or even on Vivi's, who still had all of them.

Not that he felt like it, while he was under the influence of Igah's injections.

The family had scant provisions, the two children wanted to set out at once in search of game, but the other Eskimos had already informed them that the noise of the machines, reverberating far afield, had driven away all wildlife, and almost most of the fish and seals had been avoiding these waters since the last summer, when the Company's ship had dumped engine oil—a particularly noisome kind that clung to the beach and discouraged the animals.

While Vivi and her children were building a little house of sod and stones and snow, a woman named Kio came to lend them a hand. She had already talked to Vivi while the family had been waiting outside the infirmary, and offered her a can of white men's food. Vivi couldn't accept it, of course, without first asking Papik's permission, anymore than she could give away some of the family's own food without authorization.

Kio was as broad as she was tall, with a fat face and warm manners; a real woman of Men. Of two Men, in fact—Nualik and Kutsikitsok, who found it convenient to share her, northern nomads that they were.

By and by a few other women came, to help and trade information and gossip. No one knew, nor really cared to know, what the white men were looking for at Snow White—why they drilled the permafrost with machines that were as huge as they were noisy. It must be something they had lost, or at any rate that they set great store by, for they didn't like living above the dog frontier. To get them up there, the Company had to pay them very high wages. And no one could remember ever having seem white women that far north, except in the magazines with which the workers papered the walls of their dwellings to keep out the drafts.

The family learned that the Company accused the Eskimo workers of being unreliable—which was plain slander. An Eskimo worked as well as any white man

—unless he sighted a seal or a bear, which hereabout happened rarely enough nowadays, or became tired or sleepy or bored or hungry or thirsty. Then of course he had to take time out. But whenever an Eskimo felt like working, nothing and nobody could stop him.

It was rather the Eskimos who had grounds for complaining. Like all free societies, they were not used to taking orders, but to discussing each problem with the whole group and listening to everybody's opinion. That was not the white men's way. They simply imparted orders and expected blind obedience. If an Eskimo asked for the reason or suggested a different solution, the white man became angry and, more often than not, red in the face. But the Eskimos didn't resent his outlandish manners; they would pity him, telling themselves that he was probably bad-tempered by nature and couldn't help acting the way he did.

When they found the white man's ways too hard to take, they simply harnessed their dogs and left, forfeiting their back wages in token of protest.

The Company was making every effort to retain its workers at Snow White. It had provided its main building, the Center, with a store that replenished its shelves in summer when the Company ship came in, a mess hall equipped with tables and chairs where one could listen to music and play cards and buy strong beer and weak food, and even a small sauna capable of dissolving the greasiest crust. Everything—chairs, tables, bunks, the walls themselves—had been manufactured in white man's country, and was lit with electricity produced by a machine that never stopped whirring.

What the Eskimos found hardest to digest was having to keep set hours. Since neither the wildlife nor the weather observed the clock, they had never seen the necessity for keeping time. They had hunted when hungry, gorged whenever meat was plentiful against the inevitable periods of dearth, and slept when they were tired or the weather kept them indoors, rather than when the clock told them to, as the white men did.

"Do they also laugh by the clock?" Vivi inquired, arousing loud hilarity. But not nearly as loud as the woman who answered in the affirmative.

The white men furthermore reproached the Eskimos their lack of any sense of economy, for their hearts weren't bent on settling their debts with the store, but on spending their wages as quickly as possible, and mainly on beer.

One reason the Eskimos gave for their need to drink was that the white men's working taboos were incomprehensible to them. Drinking didn't make them more comprehensible, but it helped them to stop wondering; like why there were jobs for white men only even when the Eskimos could do them better. It seemed the white workers had to belong to a union, which meant going through mysterious initiations in their home country before being allowed to perform those jobs. The Eskimos, because they had not gone through those initiations, were only assigned simple tasks, like moving heavy equipment and cleaning things or handing utensils to the foreign workers. Every white man admitted that the Eskimos picked up technical skills with fabulous ease, thanks to their practical sense and photographic memory. But the strange working taboos prevented employing them in the more difficult tasks that would have been amusing to do —at least for a little while.

The Eskimos couldn't always conceal from the foreigners what they thought of them, as when they discovered that even a white worker who did the same job that an Eskimo did was paid a higher wage. When they discovered that, some of them had to put their hands over their mouths not to laugh right out into the paymaster's face. Now here were these powerful people who flew through the clouds making a lot of noise and always calculated things with pencils and paper—and they hadn't noticed that the Eskimos did the same job better and faster and for longer hours than white men, and should therefore receive not lower but higher pay!

What a lark.

All this and more the family learned from the woman who helped them delay the building of the house with chatter. They offered to take Vivi and her children to see He Who Pays—the white man they believed to be the owner of the Company because he shelled out the money. He would surely give them work, as the Eskimos he had engaged kept deserting their jobs and he needed all the hands he could get. With the money they could buy food at the store.

Vivi said she would have to ask Papik. But there was no hurry. First she had to finish the house and then bring the garments in order; meanwhile they could eat their sled, which was soon going to thaw anyway if they couldn't move on.

The next time the doctor found Papik's entire family camped at the infirmary he made a face and instructed Igah to inform them that they would all have to take a bath before they could be admitted again.

"In that case we leave," announced Papik.

"No, you are not going to leave!" said nurse Igah, once more in a testy mood.

"But nobody's going to take a bath!"

Just as there was no end to the Eskimos' surprise over the foreign quirks, so the doctor found plenty to marvel about whenever he met Papik's family at the infirmary —like the time he saw Ootuniah stretched out stark naked on the floor, being scrubbed from head to foot by her mother with a garment scraper. Bashful in front of strangers, and especially this one, Ootuniah reached at once for a cover.

"What are you doing?" the doctor asked when he had recovered speech.

"They've advanced the date of their spring scrubbing," giggled Igah, again high on cough medicine. "To be sure to get around that bath."

"Why are they so afraid of it?"

"Because water weakens the skin."

"Superstition!" And the doctor bared his hairy forearm. "Ask this man whether my skin is weak."

Papik thumbed and probed it, and finally pronounced: "It is not strong."

The advent of summer made for uninterrupted sunshine relieved by occasional snowfall, broke up the sea crust preparing it for its southward cruise, brought clouds of screaming sea birds fishing in the dark channels between the ice pans, and swarms of bloodthirsty gnats that wrought havoc with the white men's faces but left the Eskimos' calloused skins alone—and saw the awkward courtship of the white angakok who was falling hard for the Polar girl's odd charm.

Not the least of which was the terror with which he seemed to inspire her.

While Papik remained laid up waiting for his bones to mend, his relatives became part of the camp life. He Who Pays was glad to enlist members of a family that was bound to stay on so long as its father remained tied to the ceiling of the Place Where People Undress.

This paymaster was a small but high-strung man with sandy hair and ruddy skin and a cartridge belt bristling with pencils. As he didn't speak the language, he had put one Pootoo in charge of all the natives on the Company payroll—an Eskimo who had lived among a white men's tribe below the dog frontier and had gone through their initiations and could play interpreter on a clear day.

Vivi was assigned to the mess hall, which the Eskimos called the Place Where People Get Stoned, but her work was in the kitchen which was just a small partition of the mess hall and which the Eskimos called the Place Where the Meats Get Burned. She had to help another woman, who rarely showed up, to do the heavier jobs, as it behooved women, like carrying the fuel drums for the stove and the ice for the supply of drinking water, and washing things.

As a rule, Eskimos and white men got along very well, especially when nobody got murdered. But there were some harmless little conspiracies on either side against the other, as in the case of the tableware.

The white men wanted their tableware washed with real water after each meal, as in their own country, where water was easy to come by. In Snow White it meant first hauling and then melting a lot of ice. So the women waited until no white man was looking and then followed the traditional method: they set the dirty dishes out the window, and the dogs licked them clean, doing as commendable a job as any housewife ever had.

Meanwhile a warm friendship was developing between Vivi and good fat Kio. To spend more time with her new friend, Kio often helped her work Where the Meats Get Burned, without pay. And Vivi needed the comfort of her company, since she saw little of her own family.

Ootuniah was too proud to work and spent much time at the infirmary, to console her father for his forced immobility, which made him very restless. And the doctor often asked her to lend him a hand, for Igah showed up ever less often Where People Undress and ever more Where They Get Stoned. The doctor also bade Ootuniah to stop honoring him with the title of Old Wizard and to address him by his name, which was Hendrik, but came out as Indalerak from Eskimo lips.

And yet she learned quickly the white men's tongue, which was simple enough compared to her own. More heroic was Doctor Hendrik's resolve to learn Ootuniah's language, whose intricacies usually eluded white men's grasp. But the girl seemed to attract him with the lure of the unknown, if not the fascination of the depths, and he was eager to dig into that virgin territory, regardless of difficulties and dangers.

Once he asked her to clean a knife that he used for lancing people's skins. She did it by licking it with her tongue. That launched him into a passionate lecture on hygiene, which failed to convince her, for her family shouldn't be alive if the half she understood were true. But she loved to watch his tilted, mobile nose when he spoke in anger. And when he saw her gaping at him, his earnestness would dissolve into laughter, which she would echo. Meanwhile she tried following his recommendations also when he wasn't there.

Her mother would tease her about it. But after awhile Ootuniah didn't want to talk about Indalerak anymore, and became nervous and sullen when he was mentioned.

Only Ernenek's boyish mind was fascinated without reservations by the foreign novelties, and there was little room for his family in his thoughts while he discovered the white men's world. Forever reckless, he had already experienced, within one single turn of the clock, the novelty of alcohol, tobacco, and the communal sauna, which had meant the first bath of his life.

That was not all he did. Pootoo, the Eskimo in charge of Eskimos, had assigned him to help in the hangars where the small airplanes and the big bulldozer were kept.

21

The Breaking of the Ice

"Working for others—servants!" Papik was trying to sound jocular while Vivi accompanied him home. He was hobbling on his plaster cast, with the support of a cane.

"There is no game," Vivi said. "The sea is broken. We can't travel before it freezes again. And we shouldn't before Indalerak says that your leg is well."

Papik's next move was to tear down the family's little house, built without the benefit of his directions, and to start rebuilding it properly. Meanwhile he complained that his son wasn't there to help him, as a son should and a father would.

"One was working," Ernenek explained when he showed up. "Pootoo says that at the end of the summer one can get a shotgun. Then we can kill lots of bears."

"It is not impossible that when you have your shotgun you'll need bullets," Papik said.

"One will trade hides for bullets."

"You'll need the hides for making clothes."

"One will shoot more bears and buy a nylon parka."

"And freeze to death in it." Papik tried not to sound contemptuous toward his father's soul that dwelled in his son.

"A silly boy will get still more bears and buy a stove to keep warm," Ernenek said.

"Then you'll need still more hides to buy fuel."

"Easy—with a shotgun."

Papik wrinkled his nose. "In most regions near the trading posts and the police, the white men take away your shotgun if you kill more than two bears a year, or more than a few seals. Whereas they kill more seals than anyone can count—and without bothering to return the bones to Sedna."

"There must be a reason."

"There always is. And the reason is that they are crazy. So crazy that they believe that they alone make sense. But we must not take away their beliefs. We must only keep away from them. Pardon a stupid father for telling you what he knows."

Ernenek smiled sheepishly. "Pardon a stupid son—who would like, just once, to hunt bear with a shotgun and to take a big machine for a walk."

Company regulations prohibited Eskimos at Snow White from having firearms. First there was the danger that one who had drunk too much beer would be caught by the frenzy of the Men and start firing at anyone in sight, just for the joy of noise. The other reason was that he who had a shotgun was sure to lose interest in his work and follow the lure of the hunt.

In fact not one Eskimo at Snow White had a shotgun. All who worked there wanted to buy one But they couldn't before the paymaster declared the working season closed.

Waloonga, a half-breed who ran the Company store, had a beautiful shotgun on display, as an encouragement.

It seemed it was important to the Company that the projects scheduled for the summer should be completed

on time. Certain machines had to be set up and a pier
had to be built so that next year the ships could dis-
charge their cargoes directly on land without transfer-
ring them first into small boats, as at present.

And shortly after the sea crust had broken, a Company ship came smashing through the floes with its steel
prow and unloaded a lot of goods and material and
utensils into launches, which brought them to the beach.
The ship also landed a group of white men who were
paid to work for twelve solid hours every day, seven
days a week, to make the most of the short summer.

While the ship lay anchored offshore, there was the
smell of seaweed, engine oil, and tar in the air. Snow
White became filled with noise and activity, and there
was more movement at the infirmary, too. Many workers gashed their thumbs or dropped weights on their toes
or came to blows at the Place Where People Get Stoned,
and there was also occasional knife-play.

It was an exciting period.

It was also the period when Doctor Hendrik most
needed his nurse and could least find her, for Igah preferred cavorting with white workmen that were strong
and healthy rather than attending to those that were sick
or injured. She lay in wait for them after work and went
to drink beer with them or to see how their lodgings
looked inside. Igah was neither pretty nor young, and
only pleasant when she had drunk enough beer or cough
syrup, but she was available, and this was all that the
men asked, whether white men or real Men. And Doctor Hendrik had ever more often recourse to Ootuniah,
on whom he could always rely.

Papik's resentment against the foreigners reached a
new high. They ignored him, not one of them sought his
advice, which he would have been delighted to give.
Those savages seemed indeed more interested in Vivi
than in him.

"Some women get permission to laugh with the white men," she once informed him with a shy smile.

"There's at least one woman in this camp who hasn't that permission," Papik scowled.

"White men can be nice. They give presents to the women, and sometimes money to their husbands," Vivi said temptingly.

"A stupid husband can get you all you want," Papik exaggerated. "And you are smart if you remember that."

"Of course." Vivi lowered her eyes. "Somebody just thought you ought to know."

"What about Ootuniah? You warned her?"

"She never smiled at men before. A mother was beginning to worry. But now she smiles at Indalerak, the white angakok, and at nobody else."

"A man noticed it in the Place Where People Undress. And he hopes that you gave her all the vital instructions."

"Ootuniah knows that she may not laugh with men, nor look at the moon, before she catches a husband who will take care of any child."

"Why must she smile at a foreigner, of all people?" Papik said angrily. "They have revolting diseases and lead crazy lives, in lands fit for no man."

"Ootuniah knows all that. But who can command the heart?" Vivi poked his stomach and pursed her lips: "In her youth a silly woman took a fancy to a young bear from the northern ice. Her parents kept telling her that she wouldn't want to live there. But now she wouldn't want to die anywhere else."

Papik acknowledged the declaration with a grunt and reached for his fishing gear.

A few ice pans always got blocked at the end of the beach until the pressure of new arrivals pushed the outer ones out to sea again. Papik went fishing on one of the outer pans, hoping that the currents wouldn't suddenly carry it off. But he was willing to take risks for the sake of decent food.

He used all his fishing skill and know-how. He baited the water hole with crumbs. He blew bubbles onto the surface to arouse the fish's curiosity. He kept motionless, his behind to the sky, ignoring the cramps in his injured thigh. And once he had managed to get out a fair-sized codfish.

But after the Company ship had dumped oil into the pure waters, his only catch had been a baby shark—dog food. And yet he ate some of it himself, and not just the tastiest bits like the cheeks and eyes, before letting his pack have the rest.

Then a stroke of luck enabled him to be put on the Company payroll without having to submit to the indignity of actually working. After somebody had made off with the shotgun on display in the store, and also the jars of peanut butter kept disappearing from the shelves, Papik was asked to play watchman when Waloonga rested, thus becoming the last member of the family to be gainfully employed; and without any loss of face.

The paymaster scrawled little figures in a large ledger, showing how much the Company owed to the workers and how much they owed to the store, which in turn belonged to the Company. At the end of the season, each worker would be told how much money, if any, he had coming to him. And whether it would buy a shotgun.

Papik didn't take that job to earn a shotgun, but because Waloonga had convinced him that if he caught red-handed the criminal who raided the store he was not only entitled to kill him on the spot, but by so doing he would also gain the appreciation of the white spirits, who, contrarily to the Men's spirits, regarded as sinful the appropriation of other people's provisions. Papik's hunting instincts were thereby reawakened, prompting him to whet his arrowheads and tighten his bow, before setting up a bunk in proximity of the peanut butter jars.

However, Papik's body was used to falling asleep when there was nothing really important to do, with the result that more peanut butter disappeared while he was on guard duty, entailing considerable loss of face for him and prompting him to try harder in order to regain it.

At long last his efforts were rewarded, but he was definitely going through an unlucky period, for the only sinner he caught sight of turned out to be his own son, Ernenek. So there was nothing left for Papik to do but to close again the eye he had cautiously opened and pretend that he hadn't awakened.

The sun was up all the time, and so were most of the Men, who didn't want to sleep away a good part of the short-lived summer, as the foreigners did whenever their watches told them that it was time to be tired. And it was during one of the white men's rest periods that a group of Eskimos who stood on the beach, smoking pipes and debating the state of the world, turned silent and gaped at a glittering iceberg sailing by.

Ever since the coastal pack had floated southward with the currents, the sea had been spangled with isolated floes of all sizes and shapes—from chips as small as fists to bergs as large as islands, rising hundreds of feet from sea level. Some crashed against the beach before drifting on. But the berg that caught the men's attention was different from any other they had seen that summer.

It was populated with polar bears—more than a man counted to the end.

The bears ignored Snow White; they waltzed without a care in the world over their drifting island's blue-white slopes or plunged for fish in the dark waters or took pleasure swims along the edge or rested from their labors sunning the icicles that hung from their furry bellies.

The sight of a whole clan of bears frolicking on a summer cruise fired the Men with instant hunting fever and threw the camp into a turmoil.

Ignoring Pootoo's orders not to move, the Eskimos ran for their weapons. The first ones who came back with their spears and bows tried to float the two ship launches that were beached. Members of the crew, alerted by Pootoo, came on the run to stop them, starting a fist-swinging fight.

Other Eskimos, realizing that the launches would not be available, made directly for the ice pans blocked at the end of the beach.

At that juncture the paymaster emerged from his hut, sleepy but alarmed. Donning his fur jacket over his underwear, he shouted at Pootoo to remind the men that they could not leave before their contract expired. But although Pootoo repeated the warning loud and clear and in the real language, nobody seemed to hear him.

In the course of the summer, the paymaster had discovered that all the Eskimos held Papik in great respect, even if he saw no reason for it; and he was convinced that a man who had his whole family on the payroll could be counted on to influence his brothers on the Company's behalf.

So he galloped to Papik's house, towing Pootoo along.

Papik was lying on his back after a useless fishing session and wondering what sins the family had committed to deserve such a string of misfortunes. Nobody got punished without reason. Likely as not, Vivi had kept fish and meat in one and the same pot. Sins were the women's specialty. Or the children had killed a white caribou. Or else the spirits had finally got wise and decided to take revenge on the family because Ootuniah had dared to hunt seal instead of staying indoors; but that possibility was so horrible to contemplate that he banned it at once from his thoughts. As soon as the sea froze, reopening the travel season, they would consult Ivaloo again, whose reputation as an angakok had been reported to be still spreading, no less than her offspring.

Listless and downhearted, Papik was paying no attention to the bedlam outside. But when he saw Pootoo barge in with He Who Pays and heard him babbling excitedly something about men and bears, his eyes lit up. He bounced to his feet, reached for furs and spear, and hobbled out.

He saw the iceberg full of bears. He saw Men and dogs heading for the floes detained at the end of the beach, and Ootuniah running homeward from the infirmary for her hunting gear and garments.

As to Ernenek, he had grabbed hold of Waloonga and was imploring him to let him have a shotgun without waiting for the end of the working season. The boy couldn't have chosen a worse moment. The frenzied paymaster, aided by Waloonga and Pootoo, seized and shook him and refused to let him go, wasting no breath on explanations.

Hopping from floe to floe, Kio's two husbands, Kutsikitsok and Nualik, were the first to gain the outermost ice pan and tried to separate it from its neighbors using feet and spears. The pan was scraping along the others, enabling more Men to board it before drifting free.

Hobbling on his cast and loping with the support of his spear, Papik was the last of the five who made it.

22

Benighted

With the advent of darkness, the ice had become once more the territory of the Men. Snow White lay frostbound and silent. Seabirds and airplanes had winged south. The landing strip was abandoned. The machines were hibernating, except the one that produced electric power. And nearly all the white men had returned below the trees.

Left behind were only the paymaster, in charge of Company installations, and Angakok Indalerak or Doctor Hendrik.

Nobody knew why he had remained. He had little to do. The few cases requiring his attention were burns on native thighs and buttocks—and only at the outset of winter. The Men who fished in the ice holes in the bitter cold of night covered themselves with a caribou blanket under which they kept a lamp burning—to keep warm and to make the fish believe that daylight had returned and it was time for them to come up and get speared. Usually the Men held their position either until they had speared a fish or their clothes caught fire. But as the winter progressed, the ice grew too thick to be pierced by anyone but seal and walrus, ruling out any fishing on the Men's part.

And so Doctor Hendrik didn't even have burns to treat.

There was almost no wildlife about. The occasional bears that roamed the ice were as hard to spy as the foxes that betrayed their presence mainly through their brief, regular barks that hacked the silence of the night. And apparently the seals kept shunning those waters after the Company ship had dumped more oil, for no amount of listening revealed any breathing holes.

Topping all misfortunes, Waloonga had run out of beer, as consumption during the summer had exceeded expectation. Whereafter most of the few Eskimos still remaining departed from Snow White, abandoning either their wages or their debts.

But while some went away, others arrived in this season for traveling—on sleds or with pack dogs or stamping on foot with a wife or some companions, their arched backs bulging with bundles held by a thong griding their foreheads—wanting to barter skins for weapons and tobacco and maybe something to drink.

The Eskimos were not the only resourceful race. White men had long ago revealed to the storekeeper that there were endless ways for making intoxicating brews if the need arose. And since the Company taboo against hard liquor did not apply beyond the working season, Waloonga resurrected the receipe from his memory, reached for some of the potato flour, dried fruits, sugar, and yeast on his shelves and allowed them to ferment in canisters that once had contained kerosene and added their own delicate flavor to the mash.

It was a great success.

Waloonga was the first to get drunk on it, out of honesty, to make sure it was safe. The next one was a traveler who had just arrived from afar. He guzzled it with such enthusiasm that he passed out beside his sled and was devoured by his team without ever waking up.

His misfortune made two other Men's fortunes, enabling them to leave Snow White with the victim's widow
and dogs.

The Eskimos had learned that He Who Pays didn't
own the Company, but was merely another white servant, and that his bosses below the tree line—who never
ventured this far north and were somebody else's servants—wanted to do without native labor in the coming
season, since not one of the projects scheduled for com-
pletion in the past summer had been terminated, and
somebody had to be blamed for the general debacle. So
the paymaster had blamed it on his Eskimo workers,
just because they had deserted or proved otherwise unreliable.

The Men laughed good-naturedly when Pootoo told
them this. It just went to show the extent of the foreigners' ignorance. Anybody with a bit of sense would be
happy and proud to have an Eskimo help him.

To be near the Company Center, the few that were
left lived in a communal house they had built of sod and
stones before the surface of the ground froze, instead of
moving upon the sea ice for the winter. They felt cozy
and sheltered among the mingled smells of burning oil,
drying leather, urine, whelps, human skin, and rotting
meats.

But all this was not enough comfort for Vivi.

When she woke up from her lengthening sleeps, she
would feel lost, finding herself among strangers and,
more often than not, deprived of her family. So she
leaned ever more on Kio, who felt duty-bound to be
twice as sad as Vivi, since she was missing not one but
two husbands, who had departed with Papik; not to
mention her grown son who had left Snow White earlier,
scouting for game, and had not been seen again.

Men had been orbiting around the two grass widows

ever since the husbands had left. But Vivo and Kio advised each suitor to await the husbands' return if he only wanted a quick laugh or until there was definite proof of their demise if the object was marriage. They said so mainly out of politeness. Both were confident that their husbands would be back.

There was now little to do Where the Meats Get Burned, few clothes to mend with the children leading a sedentary life, and the two ladies whiled away the time between sleeps by smoking pipes, playing cards, and drinking mash—activities Vivi had learned to appreciate from her more experienced friend. Kio had no money, as her husbands and son had kept her too busy sewing and chewing to work for the Company, but Vivi came up for all her needs, and was proud to do it.

Because her family had back wages to collect, Waloonga let her have all the mash and tobacco and canned or dried food she asked for, charging the family account and then leveling with the paymaster.

The two women were very good at pipe smoking, but had to make up new rules for the card game all the time, as nobody remembered the original rules; besides, every change added interest to the game. Meanwhile they compared their fates and counted their worries.

"The men left too suddenly, without enough dogs and equipment," Vivi would fret. "Especially the lack of the right charms could prove disastrous."

And Kio: "And not even a lamp nor a sewing kit between them, nor a woman to warm their feet or mend their clothes and boots, which by now must have sprung leaks. If they slip and dunk an arm or a leg into the water, it's the end."

"The bones of one's husband were not well yet." Vivi didn't dare pronounce Papik's name, convinced though she was that he must be alive; yet she preferred to play it safe.

Kio felt likewise, never naming Nualik and Kutsikitsok either.

"A woman's husbands are getting old," she would merely say.

"One's husband is getting much older," Vivi would reply to cheer her up. "Apart from being a cripple."

"No, no! A woman's husbands are older. And shaky. But please don't tell anybody."

So it went for interminable sessions of pipe smoking and card playing, until Waloonga's mash made them forget the absent dear ones and put them to sleep, their cheeks resting on the scattered cards.

Ootuniah was getting more and more nervous. At times she was so irritable when at home that her mother wished her back in the Place Where People Undress. But then her mood could change with the suddenness of the arctic weather, as the time when she confided to her mother, beaming like the rising sun:

"It is not impossible that a girl would like to have a child."

Vivi stared at her. "Once you thought children were just messy and a general bother."

"Aren't they?"

"Sure. Look at yourself."

It ended in a guffaw and an embrace.

Ootuniah found her life at the infirmary disturbing and interesting at the same time. It was interesting mainly because it was disturbing. Doctor Hendrik had asked her to replace Igah permanently, as the nurse had vanished from Snow White, probably with a departing sled.

Ootuniah wasn't only learning how to treat sore thumbs and to speak Doctor Hendrik's language while teaching him her own; she was also learning, without anybody's advice, how to look ever less like a boy and more like a girl. She still let her long, lank hair fall on her shoulders, as the men did, but now she combed it with care, like a woman.

It was the first time in her life that she was worrying about her appearance, and she still didn't know what to make of the slightly cross-eyed image that gazed back at her from the mirror. Was she really as ravishing as Doctor Hendrik said, poking her little flat nose or following the design of her slightly raised lips with his smooth finger? It was not impossible, even if nobody else had told her so. Her people never extolled a girl's looks in her hearing, in order not to embarrass her.

She was intrigued and also frightened by the stirrings the nearness or merely the thought of Doctor Hendrik caused in her. They were not sexual. At least so she believed, because sex held few mysteries for one grown in the intimacy of the igloos.

What puzzled and disturbed her was the turmoil in her heart.

23

Love Story

Before the night sent the fish bunking in the depths, Ootuniah had once taken Doctor Hendrik fishing on the sea ice. She had already made him shave off his little beard for the winter, lest it accumulate ice that could freeze his face, advising him to let it grow back in summer, to frighten off the gnats.

It was the first time Doctor Hendrik saw her in her element, crouching as motionless as a snowman over the hole she had chiseled in the ice. After she had hissed her disapproval because he had dared to stir, he remained stock still, stoically; until she plunged her three-pronged spear into the water and promptly lifted it again, aquiver with a black salmon that had barely time to gasp before freezing into stillness. He watched her suck with relish an eye out of its socket, but refused, with thanks, her offer of the other eye.

After that fishing session, Doctor Hendrik had to wait several turns of the clock before he knew that he wouldn't have to forego his nose, severely frostbitten despite the blubber Ootuniah had smeared on it. And from then on he preferred learning more about her life while staying indoors.

"Please, never ask me what we do in our igloos,"

Ootuniah told him once with one of her shy, fleeting smiles.

"Why?"

"There are too many things that a silly girl doesn't like or can't understand about your life. How could you understand ours?"

Nurtured inside a small and exclusive group, she combined the curiosity of a bear with a bear's diffidence. But this white man, though a powerful angakok, seemed so understanding and eager to please her that she felt flattered and moved, and with him she came out of her shell more than she ever had with her own family. The very strangeness that appalled her also attracted her. His hands were pale and soft, like a baby's; comical on a grown man. No scars, no calluses, no cracks, no broken nails; only chilblains. She preferred not to think what a harpoon shaft would do to those palms if he should ever try to hang on to a seal, let alone a walrus, struggling under water. Another oddity that fascinated and disgusted her at the same time was the hairiness she saw on his forearms and that she supposed extended to his whole body, as in the devil. In spite of everything and although he wasn't a great hunter, he affected her strongly. She recoiled when his hand brushed her.

And yet she couldn't remain long without seeing him, and much less without admitting him into her thoughts.

Before the last airplane left, he had asked her whether she would go away with him. She was astonished. He should know that she needed her father's consent.

"I shouldn't say this," Doctor Hendrik had remarked at that point. "But I doubt your father will return."

She glared at him with her glacier-blue eyes. "It is not impossible that you are mistaken, Indalerak."

"So I hope."

And that was that for the time being. But in the heart

of night, when even a flat and well-greased nose couldn't shrug off the bite of frost, Ootuniah picked up that exchange where it had been left off.

"If he gets cold or runs out of food, he can always build a shelter and go into hibernation," she said abruptly, while they were puttering in the Place Where People Undress.

"Who?"

"My father."

"Human beings don't hibernate, Ootuniah! Only a few animals do that. Like the bears."

Ootuniah put her hand on Doctor Hendrik's arm and smiled up into his comical face. "Pardon a stupid girl for contradicting a wise oldster, but you are so ignorant. On the ice, the bears are the only animals that don't hibernate. The Men do."

"How?"

"When we have not enough provisions to last through the winter, we stop eating altogether and let our bodies cool. It is a strange but also delicious feeling. Slowly, when they have cooled down, our bodies float off to sleep. Sometimes we wake up in the middle of the winter night, shaking. It is a warning—that the body has burned up so much fat and flesh that it's about to freeze and die. Then we put some blubber and snow in our mouths to melt and go back to sleep. When the light of spring wakes us up, our clothes have grown much too large. If the warning in the body fails to work, the others find a corpse in the igloo."

"Have you done it?"

"Often. And without ever finding a corpse," she laughed.

"Are you not afraid of going to sleep without knowing if you'll wake up?"

"Why? Sooner or later we all go to sleep without waking up. It's easier in the igloo than outside."

"Do many people do it?"

"All those from the northern ice. And many water people, too. Unless they have small children. Children are too stupid to wake up before they freeze."

"But then," Ootuniah told Doctor Hendrik at another time, her thoughts always harking back to her father, "it almost never happens that in a group everybody dies."

"Why?"

"In the water a whole group might die at the same time. On the ice, it seldom happens. If one man dies, the others can eat him and get warm through him. And my father is certainly not going before the others."

"You must be joking!"

Doctor Hendrik looked so horror-struck that it made Ootuniah laugh.

"Why? Is it better that all die, or that some live?"

"Don't tell me you have eaten human flesh!"

"We never had to. But my mother's father did. She has it from him that man tastes like bear, but better."

As Doctor Hendrik remained speechless, she poked his chest with her finger and said: "Now you must put a question."

"What?"

"You heard that man tastes better than bear. So you should ask: Does woman taste better than man?"

He joined in her laughter then, hoping, but not believing, that it was all a big joke, and asked: "Well? Does woman taste better than man?"

"Find out."

That was the first time he kissed her. Her teeth, eaters of raw meat, gleamed so alluringly in the radiant face which had not yet lost all the copper from the summer sun that he clasped her in his arms and pressed a kiss on her smile.

She hesitated during a few quickening heartbeats before she threw back her head, smashed her stony little fist between his eyes, and spat into his face.

Like the well-bred girl that she was.

"How many are there, people from the ice? Who live like you?"

"Who knows? Many more than a man counted to the end. We only know the names."

"Tell me the names. I'll tell you the number."

At first she liked his game. "There is Kanuk, Nasak, Ookalik, Orpa, Intedi. And Nuga and Odin and Ippi and Mekiana and Igadaghik and Simigak and Uvdloriak and Avatak. There is Nualik and Kutsikitsok who happened to be here in camp. And Ekeluk and Serkok and Kiviyok and Angutivdluarsuk and Panik." She went on until she ran out of names, and she was sure she hadn't forgotten many.

"That makes over eighty men," said Doctor Hendrik, who had been counting by magic, without resorting to his fingers and toes. "Do they all have a wife?"

"No. Some only have half a wife, like Nualik and Kutsikitsok who share Kio."

"Do all have children?"

"No. But a few have two. Like we."

"That makes above two hundred of you. Is it all that's left of the Polar men?"

"We never were many more. Nor many less."

"How do you know?"

"Everybody knows that. On the ice that never melts, there is very little game—some seal and bear. Only so many men can live on them."

"The others die?"

"Or move south and become water people, who are ice bound only three seasons out of four." But Ootuniah was not deeply interested in numbers. "Now tell me, Indalerak—where would you take me? Among the trees, where the Men pine and die?"

Doctor Hendrik wasn't able to answer this. He knew that Ootuniah's people couldn't live below the tree line; that one ran anywhere into members of every race, but into real Men only above the tree line, for abroad they died. All he could say at present was that he would hate to leave without her, and her astonishment grew.

"A silly girl won't like leaving you either," she said. "But you can't travel with us. You are useless. And when you drop into a hole and drown, a girl will be very, very sad."

Doctor Hendrik was reflecting. "You think I could get used to the cold? And to live like you?"

"Some do, some don't. Who can tell?"

"You must know that for my own people I am a northerner. From the very edge of the tree line."

"That's very far south!"

"Far north for us. We hunt caribou in the summer. But in the winter we stay mostly in warm houses."

"You can learn to love the cold. There is nothing worse but also nothing better. Listen, Indalerak. In the winter we starve for the sun and yearn for all the meat and excitement it brings. But when the air becomes warm and full of insects and there is water everywhere, we feel bad and can't wait for the sun to go home and the sea to freeze. Maybe what my father says is true."

"What does he say?"

"That the white men keep traveling in strange lands because they look for the best place to live. We don't— we have found it."

"He may be right!"

"But if the white men don't like the cold, why do you all keep coming?"

"Few really do. Some because they earn more. Others although they earn less—wanting to help. I mean, our

men who come north include some of our best and some
of our worst. You understand?"

"No. Why did *you* come?"

"Because I could make more money here. But now
that I've known you, I would rather help than make
money."

"A stupid girl still doesn't understand. Who you want
to help?"

"You. And your people."

"A girl likes you because you make her laugh so
much. *We* must help *you* all the time. Pardon me, but
you don't even know how to hunt and fish."

"Life doesn't consist only of eating!"

"Of course not. But mostly," Ootuniah said soberly.

"Is where your next meal comes from all you ever ask
yourselves?"

"What else should we ask?"

Doctor Hendrik exploded. "Where we all come from!
Who made the stars. And why. Things like that."

Ootuniah looked surprised. "But we know all this.
Don't you?"

"No. Not really."

"You are making fun of me, Indalerak!"

"No, Ootuniah. We don't know for sure a single one
of the important things."

"And you sit around, without trying to find out?"

"We try to."

"Why don't you ask us?"

"Well, tell."

"Listen well, Indalerak, so you can instruct your people. Once when the frozen ocean broke open with a big
bang, the noise created the Black Raven. As he didn't
know what to do with himself, he started making little
men from ice. The men, wanting to have somebody to
scold, made women from little clumps of sod. As the
Raven couldn't see them in the winter night, he made

two lamps—Father Moon and Mother Moon, and sent them traveling from east to west. Mother Moon soon got bored escorting her husband and went south instead, to see what the Sun was doing. So the Raven hacked her into little pieces—and that's where the stars come from. You smile! Don't you believe it?"

"Why not? It makes at least as much sense as what our own angakoks tell us."

Since accidents were in abeyance, like everything else, during the midwinter frost, their conversations were seldom interrupted. But this one was—by a group that carried in an unconscious, cyanotic Vivi.

She had hanged herself.

Nothing had allowed foreseeing her gesture. She had been doing her reduced work and leading her accustomed life with her usual smiling gentleness, and kept smiling throughout her suicide attempt, and beyond.

Some people in the communal house were sleeping, but others were in the Place Where One Gets Stoned, and when two of these had returned home, reeling from too much mash, they saw Vivi hanging from the ceiling like a huge bat, her toes scraping the floor. So they had hastened to wake up everybody and to carry her to the Place Where People Undress, for if she died indoors, the house would have to be abandoned and a new one would have to be built.

"Give her your breath," Doctor Hendrik ordered Ootuniah, gathering his secret instruments and preparing to do his exorcisms.

He had taught Ootuniah some of his witchcraft, like transfusing one's own lifebreath to people who had lost theirs. Eerie. But Ootuniah was afraid of nothing if it could bring her mother back to life. So she pinched Vivi's nose to prevent the ghost escaping if it was still in her, put her own lips to her mother's, and gave her all she had, while Doctor Hendrik squirted one of his magic fluids into Vivi's vein.

At long last Vivi coughed feebly and opened her eyes, and Ootuniah fell around her neck, snuffed her and rubbed noses, and bathed her mother's face in tears. At this, Vivi frowned and pushed her away, ordering:

"Don't cry!"

"First tell me why you did it, little one!" Ootuniah said.

"When you stop crying, little one."

Ootuniah stopped and Vivi told.

"A woman has no reason to live. Father keeps coming to her in her dreams. He must be dead."

"He used to come in your dreams also before he went away."

"But now there is pain when he appears."

"Because you miss him, little one," Ootuniah said.

"The ice has long been transitable now. So why doesn't he come back?"

"He will. He is not the one to be eaten by some stupid bear or swallowed by some stupid hole. You know that."

"But what you don't know, little one, is that sometimes a mother wishes he couldn't come back."

"That's impossible!" exclaimed Ootuniah. "Why?"

"What will he say if he finds us all so changed? When you come home, you smell of soap and water, and worse. Ernenek of tobacco and firewater—if he comes home at all. Just like a silly mother. And she has discovered that her son goes bathing in the sauna, behind her back! And he seldom bothers to answer her except to tell her that she knows nothing."

"A girl will smack him so hard across the mouth that it will cry out in pain each time he opens it!"

Vivi smiled wanly. "You know you can't beat him.

He has your grandfather's name. Father wouldn't, should he ever come back."

"He *will* come back!" Ootuniah said it twice, very forcefully and stamping her foot.

As if she didn't believe it.

24

Where the Bears

Of the five men that had gone off after the bear berg, only two returned to Snow White.

Sailing on floating ice in pursuit of bear is not free of risk. A storm may topple the floe, drowning all aboard. Or Queen Sedna, who is generous since she provides all the good fish but can also be as naughty as any old woman, may send the floe to dissolve in warm southerly waters instead of following the circular currents of the North.

Endowed with a knowledge surpassing that of man, the bears desert a carrier when it becomes unsafe, and swim to shore or to a better berg, thumbing their noses at the pursuers. But what real Man wouldn't gladly risk coming to such a wet end for the sake of a bear hunt—life's greatest thrill?

To survive during the first turns of the sun, the five out of Snow White had had to eat one of their few dogs, which were all inferior specimens. The best had been busy elsewhere at the moment of departure. Noonah, for one, was battling several rivals for the favors of a bitch in heat.

Offshore, the waters around the floe were boiling with halibut and cod, but high seas were running, and while the men were trying to spear themselves a meal, lying flat on their stomachs, the sea swept over them, forcing them to move centerward.

The floe was faster than the bear berg and governable to a degree, according to where the men stood to catch the gale. By the time they boarded the berg, men and dogs were so hungry that the smell of all those bears caused their mouths to water. However, the bears were glutted with fish and unwilling to fight. The men and dogs chased some up and down the steep inclines, but kept slipping, until they came to a stop, with their tongues hanging out.

The men had specially saved a piece of meat from the slaughtered dog. They primed it with a tightly coiled strip of whalebone shaved off one of their weapons, and tossed it to the bears. Several sniffed at this bait before one obliged the hunters by swallowing it. When the first blood appeared in the bear's droppings, the men resumed the chase, but it took another two sunturns before their quarry was too weak to outrun them.

After the bear had been slain and quartered, Nualik, one of Kio's husbands and a natural worrier, tried to spoil everybody's appetite by pointing out that the worsening gale was threatening to drive the berg away from the safe circular currents.

But Papik cut him short. "First eat—then worry," he grinned with his mouth full of liver, and everybody agreed, eating as much as would go down, to postpone worrying. And no one forgot the traditional politeness while dividing choice parts, with such compliments as "After you—if there's any left."

They forgot altogether to worry and even ignored the cutting gale after stoking up until they were ready to pass out. Some of them did. One Amainalik slept so soundly that he rolled over the berg's edge and into the sea. He woke up everybody with his shouts for help while struggling in the waves, but all that his companions could do was to wave back at him.

All those who see a man drowning are confronted with a cruel dilemma. If they rescue him, they antagonize the old Sea Queen, who is entitled to her victims; if they let him drown, they may offend his family. Fortunately the iceberg's course could not be reversed, so the four huntsmen were spared the embarrassing choice; and they were doubly lucky in that they were scudding along at such a brisk pace that they were probably outrunning the dead man's shade.

Though there was some discussion as to just how fast a soul could swim in a stormy ocean.

Before the sun had come full circle above the horizon, the four had no leisure to worry about the dead. The human presence made the bears too nervous to go on fishing, and when they grew hungry enough they overcame their natural diffidence of man and started closing in. Some bears circled the four, others merely sat watching them with sly, bloodshot eyes, blowing fishy steam into their faces.

The dogs, usually spoiling to get at bears, were replete with the left overs of the kill and pretended to be busy elsewhere, proving once more that letting them eat their fill had been a mistake.

Brandishing their spears, the men took up the defensive position they had learned from the musk oxen, and disposed themselves as a four-leaf clover. Of course, the musk oxen were right. But among the Men there was always one who wanted to emerge over his peers. Papik was restrained by his cast and injury. But Kutsikitsok, the other husband of Kio, who was the oldest of the lot and should have known better, resolved all at once to prove his manliness—perhaps because he was losing it. Roaring, he broke out of formation. But his intended

quarry ducked the spear and slapped down the hunts-
man, who then was promptly bitten in the groin by another besieger, clawed and disfigured by a third, and
dragged off to a quieter spot by a fourth.

To the three remaining huntsmen's great relief, the
entire bear club retired to the berg's highest peak, to
feast undisturbed on Kutsikitsok while keeping his companions under surveillance. The men chose to sulk at
the beasts, and swapped memories of more successful
bear hunts, veritable massacres of bears, speaking loudly
to make the beasts feel properly abashed. But the bears
pretended not to hear them.

When the berg eventually thundered alongside a field
of coastal pack, the huntsmen transferred to it quickly,
leaving the bears to their summer cruise.

With best wishes.

If getting away from humdrum family life had been
easy, the way back was much less so. The surviving trio
—Papik, Nualik, and one Kigutikak—found neither
seals nor driftwood along the coast. They only spotted a
walrus patch that was out of reach without a boat.
Trekking inland with the few dogs left, they bagged
some fox and musk ox and small deer.

Under the continual sun, the men perspired abun-
dantly. The rugged ground, moist from the melted snow,
seemed to perspire as well. Among the dwarf vegetation
and wind-polished boulders, an infinity of little lakes,
ponds, and puddles had formed, and brooks as tortuous
as a wolverine's brains. The mossy carpeting of many
shades—from the creamy caribou-lichen to the brownish
peat moss—was sparsely stitched with yellow poppies,
red niviarsiak, and blue erika; rich blossoms on stunted
stalks. The men picked some green moss, to dry and use
as wicks instead of dog droppings and as insulation in
their boots instead of dog hair.

In the abrupt frost of fall, they headed back to the coast with their dogs loaded down with quarters of a large caribou as building material for a sled. But by the time they reached the frozen ocean, they were so hungry that the sled was eaten up before it was started.

To Papik's great relief, his plaster cast cracked and left him around that time. Laughter almost broke up his two companions on seeing his leg come out thin and crooked and his limp worse than before.

After building a sled with split fish, they hit pack ice while darkness was closing in. The dogs were insufficient to pull them over uneven ground, and they wintered in a snow shelter, after trapping a few foxes and locating some animal's cache of birds and eggs. They weren't familiar with the region, and the extension of the pack ice kept them stranded on a coast when spring broke the sea crust.

After they had caught a walrus, things looked brighter, but not for long. Tempers began running short when they had to spend more time doing women's work—making needles from bird bones and thread from walrus sinew and mending their own battered clothes—than hunting. And Kigutikak became so tired of always having to sit down and reason every problem out with his companions that once he tramped off growling.

And was never seen or heard of again.

When Papik rejoined Snow White with Nualik, he was still limping; he had thinned in face and body, his clothes were in dire shape, but he was in a happy, exuberant mood. By then the sun had once more sunk below the horizon but was still briefly shedding some light upon the top of the world at each turn.

The bear hunters had been away well over a year; the Company ship had paid its usual call, once more sullying the waters and restoring the supply of beer; the last airplane had left; and Snow White was girding for another long, silent night.

Papik's high spirits were short-lived. He didn't resent unduly the disappearance of all his utensils and weapons that he had left behind and that had cost him considerable labor; anything that wasn't actually in use could be appropriated by others. What angered him was that his wife and daughter could give him only a hurried welcome in the communal house, and that his son was too busy to show up at all.

Vivi was expected Where the Meats Get Burned, Ootuniah was still playing sorcerer's apprentice in the Place Where People Undress, and Ernenek was occupied in the House Where the Machines Get Tamed. It looked indeed as if only Noonah, his lead dog, had time for him.

During the past working season, the only Eskimos on the Company payroll had been the three members of Papik's family, for they could be trusted not to desert Snow White so long as they awaited his return. The paymaster hoped that this would be forever, and for them he had made an exception to the new Company rule against engaging Eskimo labor. By the same token he would also have taken on Kio, but the fat woman had refused to be harnessed into regular work so long as Vivi kept her.

While Vivi and Ootuniah were informing Papik of these events, Kio also was in the communal house, not knowing how to manifest joy over one of her husband's homecoming and at the same time advertise grief over the loss of the other. And Vivi couldn't advise her, having difficulties of her own with Papik.

"Pootoo can explain to you that it isn't shameful accepting the white men's money and food in return for our work,' she was telling him.

Ootuniah said: "There are many things we can learn from them."

Papik scoffed at this notion. "What have you learned?"

"It's important to wash ourselves all the time because the air and our bodies are full of little animals—so little they can be seen only with magic instruments—that give us diseases and pain."

Papik guffawed in derision. "Hoh! The silliest superstition ever! Disease and pain don't come from invisible little animals but from evil spirits that our angakoks can see very well."

Ootuniah dared contradict her father. "If one kills the little animals in time, one doesn't get sick."

"But we don't get sick, little one—so long as we stay away from the foreign spirits! And Ernenek?"

"He has almost learned how to tame machines. And he got a shotgun at the end of the working season."

Papik frowned. "A shotgun?"

"Yes. That he takes everywhere. Even to bed."

Papik got up, to hide his anger and retain his smile. "Any more bad news?"

"Yes," confessed Ootuniah, hanging her head and gazing at the floor. "A silly girl wishes to marry Indalerak, the white angakok."

Papik turned a big grin on Vivi. "A man's ears don't serve him well anymore. Should he go off to die?"

"You heard right," said Vivi. "Ootuniah was waiting for your consent. And you can't deny it."

Papik gazed incredulously from Vivi to Ootuniah. He shifted on his feet, swallowed hard, and his eyes began flooding.

Aghast, Vivi clutched his arm. "Papik! You are not crying?!"

"Crying? Laughing!" And he burst out roaring. "Ha ha ha! Think of all we did! Ho ho! A man lost three fingers for this child. Ha ha! You bent your back trundling her, you laughed yourself bowlegged to keep her husband happy, you wore out your teeth and eyes to make her clothes. And now she leaves us! Ho ho!" Irresistible.

Ootuniah fell around her father's neck and sniffed at his cracked old face.

"That's why a girl was not happy for a long time," she said. "Her heart didn't wish to leave you for a stranger. At the same time she knew she couldn't do without him."

"Poor world! He is no hunter. He is weak and ignorant and has an ugly smell!"

"He must be to her liking, not to your liking," Vivi reminded him.

"He must have cast a spell on her. With one of his injections."

"A silly girl keeps telling him that," Ootuniah said. "Near him she trembles. But Indalerak says it's the other way—that she cast a spell on him. He was to return below the trees, where another girl waits for him, for they both are from a sedentary tribe. But now he would like to remain in the North. He says there is somebody here he doesn't want to leave. We may go to caribou country together—because a girl who is a girl can no longer seal but can still hunt caribou."

Papik thought he had had his fill of bad news. But only until Ernenek arrived, with a nylon parka thrown carelessly on his shoulders and a shotgun in his hand.

The boy beamed on seeing his father and the two shook hands, holding them high and lowering their heads—Ernenek out of respect for his father, Papik for his own father's soul that dwelled in his son.

"He has grown!" Papik cried. "And looks like a man's father. Same eyes. Same chin. Same chest."

"He is taller than Ootuniah," said Vivi. "And still growing."

"Ernenek, you don't have to work for the white men anymore," Papik said. "The sea is frozen, the light is right, the season for traveling. We move on."

Ernenek frowned. "A stupid boy likes to listen to loud music in the Place Where People Get Stoned."

This time Papik didn't laugh. "And he drinks firewater and eats from cans—and probably washes with hot water and soap?"

"And with steam, in the sauna," Ernenek confessed. "But meanwhile he learns things, and it is not impossible that sometime he will take for walks the same machine that broke your bones."

"You don't want to go back where the bears come from? You prefer a white men's camp?"

"No, no! But one wants to learn more about machines. Some can even fly to the moon."

"Our angakoks have been doing it all the time."

"But they won't tell me how to do it. The white men will."

"Surely Ivaloo also will tell you," Papik said. "But know that serious doubts exist about the white men's visits to the moon. It seems all they have to show is pictures, which are fakes."

"Why?"

"Not one of our angakoks has ever found the slightest trace of their angakoks on the moon. Not even their droppings. Nualik is sure of that. His brother-in-law told him so."

"A stupid nobody still wants to take that big machine around," Ernenek said stubbornly. "Just once."

"Let us wait until then," Vivi told Papik. "It seems the men soon get bored with machines and go back to hunting. Then we can leave."

"Somebody else knows that after staying too long

with foreigners many Men become too weak to leave,"
Papik said. "We go now."

Vivi bit her lip. "There is something else you ought to
know. We promised to work here all through the coming
season, for we didn't know when you'd be back. On the
say-so of He Who Pays, Waloonga let Ernenek have his
shotgun and this real nylon parka."

"Ernenek didn't pay with his wages?"

"His wages went for beer and food and tobacco. And
a silly woman also took many things she still has to pay
for."

"We give it all back."

"The beer she and Kio drank? The tobacco they
smoked? The peanut butter they ate? She also bought
food for the dogs when they seemed about to devour
one another."

"Nobody can hold a Man!" Papik announced. "Ernenek will return his shotgun and leave."

"Not right now." Ernenek avoided his father's eyes,
but his tone was firm.

"We are too old to go without a son," Vivi said.

"Too old?" Papik echoed indignantly. "He Who Pays
twisted your minds! Where is he?"

"Where people get stoned," Ernenek said.

"A man will talk to him!" Excited, Papik started getting dressed and Vivi started getting scared.

"Take care! You know what happens if you hurt
white men or break their furniture."

"A stupid man knows everything!" Papik roared.

One heartbeat ahead of him, Vivi snatched his spear,
which was his only weapon left, broke it over her knee,
flung the two halves to the ground, and spat on them for
good measure. But taking notice of a woman's deeds is
beneath a real Man.

So Papik rushed out of the house, ignoring her.

25

The First Men

He Who Pays was sitting with all his pencils in the Place Where People Get Stoned, puffing on a pipe, quaffing beer from a can, and listening to music from a box. So were Doctor Hendrik and Waloonga. Though their watches were frozen for the duration, they knew from the radio that it was time to be thirsty. And there were also the few Eskimos that were left at Snow White, including old Pootoo.

"Who advised Ernenek not to leave with his father?" Papik demanded of him on arriving, trailed by his family and Nualik and Kio. "Ask He Who Pays!"

"No need to ask," Pootoo said without taking the pipe out of his mouth. He was red-eyed and heavy-lidded, as if he had had enough to drink. "This man did. And you also had better work for us, Papik. You are too old to go back."

Papik flushed. An old man calling him old! The only proper reply was a butt in the mouth. All Pootoo could do was hastily remove his pipe before Papik's head crashed in his face and slammed him against the wall. The bystanders seized Papik just in time to be too late and held him fast. But he was satisfied that he had made his point.

Pootoo hoisted himself up, squinted at the trickle of blood from his nose, and spat out a mouthful of black toothchips, arousing the hilarity of every real Man. Pootoo himself greeted the sight of his own teeth on the floor with an embarrassed little snicker.

Unimpressed by Papik's performance, Doctor Hendrik told him: "Somebody also thinks that at your age the South is safer than the North." He surprised Papik by using the Men's own language.

"Where everybody is somebody's servant? No! A man born on the ice will die on the ice."

"You speak to him, Pootoo," Doctor Hendrik said.

Pootoo spat out some more blood and chips, passed his tongue over his lips, and turned to Papik.

"If we find our way to the town near the tree line, the Supreme Police there will see to it that we won't starve." He was lisping through his stumped teeth, causing another round of manly laughter. "The oldsters receive after each sleep a small gift of food."

"But no seal," Papik pointed out, causing gales of laughter, for he had managed to imitate Pootoo's brand-new lisp.

"But sometimes whale or caribou. And when we lose our teeth, we get new ones."

"Then you should go," Papik chuckled.

"It is not impossible that a man will."

Papik suddenly recalled the handful of similar old Men who used to sit on a bench in Aage's town, busy watching the seasons go by while waiting for the government's dole.

"And there," Pootoo went on, "your son could buy weapons and gear on credit, and pay in time with the pelts and blubber he'll get with them. And he can send his own son to the House Where the Children Sit. They learn to speak like foreigners, to count higher than a man to the end, and other white magic." Pootoo turned to Doctor Hendrik. "He heard all this before, but his head is hard as ice."

"Compliments leave me cold, Pootoo," Papik said. "Now a man has talked enough and listened too much."

He started for the exit, but Doctor Hendrik stopped him.

"Papik! Know that somebody wants to take your daughter for a wife."

"Who wouldn't? Women are scarce."

"No, no, that's not the reason!" Doctor Hendrik said with a laugh. "There are enough girls below the trees. But none like your daughter. For me, it's Ootuniah or no one. And for her sake, somebody would even live forever up here in the North."

"Is it true?"

"It is not impossible," Doctor Hendrik said. "But first one would like to help you."

"A man needs no help!"

"Everyone needs help, Papik. And for your own sake, nobody at Snow White will let you have anything. So you can't leave."

Waloonga also made himself heard. "Your wife has splurged in your absence, Papik! And now you must come up for it."

"Working!" gloated Pootoo.

Nualik gave Papik his support. "A man who wants a new partner would leave with you and Kio, but we must wait here for our son."

"A man wants no partner!"

Papik shoved everybody out of his way and stepped into the autumn.

It was gloomy out, with the foggy grayness, verging on black in the North, that heralded the night. And it was not warm. The breath was white, and a gale blew in gusts that cut like knives, but they glanced off the well-greased leather of Papik's face.

He kicked his way across the usual snarling, steaming, tail-wagging mass forever in wait for dirty dishes to lick or someone who would step out to relieve himself, and everybody else followed, putting on their furs. Excitements were a rare treat at Snow White, and mostly confined to occasional airplane crashes, which could be monotonous in the long run. Even Kio had forgotten both her joy and her sorrow, and was eager to witness the tug-of-war between Papik who wanted to leave and the others who wanted to detain him.

"You haven't even got a knife!" Vivi shouted, bowing to the wind and fighting tears. "Nor a son. Nor all your fingers. And you limp!"

Papik was paying no attention to her, but Ernenek told his mother:

"Don't fear, little one. Father is too old to travel alone. But not old enough to want to die."

Papik was breathing in deeply the smell of winter, relishing the exhilarating coldness that rushed into his lungs, expanding them hard against his ribs; deep breathing being the readiest remedy against cold, as the increased oxygen stirs the blood, generating instant warmth.

Another means is harnessing the frost to one's own service.

Indicating the dog sticks by the exit, he told Vivi to protect him from the pack. Then, before the two white men's unbelieving eyes, he lowered his pants and squatted, turning his buttocks to the crowd. Vivi triumphed as she kept the dogs away with the threat of the stick.

"See?" she laughed. "You can't even do *that* without a silly woman's help."

Hammering his fuming catch with his fists, Papik flattened it to a knifelike shape, endeavoring to work faster

than the all-pervading frost. Then he straightened up
and, facing the onlookers, he took a leak. Steaming and
crackling, his water formed an instant stalagmite of brilliant, amber ice that came nipping at the source. He
gripped the sharply pointed cone at the base, caught a
dog with the other hand, and stabbed its throat with the
icy dagger. The animal's yowl died quickly in a gurgle of
blood.

In the same way he slaughtered a second dog.

Then he melted in his mouth a handful of snow
scraped from the wind crust and squirted it upon the
blade fashioned from his organic matter, glazing it with
an ice crust that he whetted with the warmth of his naked palm. He strove for precision while racing against
the frost. Whatever was not breathing turned quickly
stiff and unwieldy. After testing the blade's edge by tip-
ping his tongue, he skinned the dog's carcasses, cutting
and pulling at the hides for all he was worth.

"What is he doing?" Doctor Hendrik asked Ootuniah.

"Building a sled. Anything will do. Even a man's
body."

"Will he really try to leave?"

"Even if it costs him his life."

"But it will!"

Ootuniah resented this. "Have you forgotten? Once
you said he would not come back."

However tightly rolled and glazed with ice, frozen dog
skins don't make smooth runners if not coated with
ivory; but it was all Papik had. On the other hand,
he required no better crossbars than the cuts of dog
meat that he welded to the runners by spraying more
melted snow upon the meeting points.

Among the pack, Noonah was awaiting its master's
commands, surrounded by followers and subjects. Papik
recognized some former members of his team that had
grown estranged and had joined the roaming dogs in his

absence. But whoever feeds me is my master, and Papik won five of them back with samples of the fresh dog meat. He hitched this team to the sled with strips of dog skin knotted together, keeping them short, to save time and material. He had nothing to load on the sled but the remnants of the slain dogs—and his own self.

When all was ready, his tension abated and he strolled toward his son, managing to swagger despite his limp.

"You won't come?" he asked.

"Yes," said Ernenek, meaning No. It meant: "Yes, you are right, I won't come." And the boy clasped his shotgun to his bosom.

"Then you can't call yourself Ernenek anymore," Papik said calmly. "A father takes back the name he gave you."

While Ernenek stood transfixed, in stunned amazement, Vivi said:

"A woman won't go without her son."

Papik glared at her, speechless. He swept the circle around him. Everybody looked grim, unmoving.

"Hah!" he snorted. "Who needs a woman? A man only wants dogs."

He was wrong and he knew it. Nobody knew better than he that in the arithmetic of arctic life the smallest unit was the couple. But he couldn't acknowledge it, with all those eyes riveted on him in fascination. He had never felt prouder of being a Man, never more defiant of everybody and the world, and ready for the impossible.

"Papik!" Vivi pleaded. "The only females you can find up there are among the bears—and they will eat you."

He brushed her off. He had seen Ootuniah in tears, clinging to her Indalerak. He hadn't seen her cry since the time she was a little girl and her family wanted to

leave her with Ivaloo. He limped over to remind her
that she mustn't. Ootuniah wept harder and fell into his
arms. He turned her around with her back to the gale.

"If you must cry, at least don't cry against the wind,"
he told her. "The tears can freeze inside the little tunnels
and burst your eyes wide open." He grinned: "And now
you know why we must learn never to cry, little one.
Not even in anger."

He took the dog stick out of Vivi's hand and swag-
gered leisurely to his sled. Noonah had been cuffing its
teammates and snapping at them, but had a hard time
keeping them in line, until Papik cracked down on them
and they started pulling, yapping after the white steam
from their muzzles, surrounded by a handful of whelps.

When the sled stopped jolting on the coastal strip and
started dancing on the smooth sea ice, Papik jumped on
a crossbar. But he was bumped and tumbled off almost
at once, for Vivi had got on too, and the sled was just a
little one, built for one man.

"You want what?" he cried, hobbling alongside.

"If you need nobody, a silly woman needs somebody!"

"We haven't enough dogs for two."

"We will."

While Papik trotted along pigeon-toed, Vivi bit morsels off the dog meat they carried and dropped them in
their wake, calling "Food!" behind her, and soon a
whole pack was trailing them.

"So!" she exulted. "What would you do without a silly woman?"

"Ride instead of run!" Papik grinned back.

Meanwhile Ernenek should have been ignoring his
parents' departure. But he didn't. Nor could all the others take their eyes off the shaggy couple and team racing for the night with a makeshift sled.

No one can tell what passed in the boy's mind at that

juncture. Whether the amazement or secret admiration he had noticed in the white men's gaze aroused his pride in the familiar life that was leaving him behind. Or whether he wanted back his grandfather's name. Everybody only saw what he did.

He flung his unpaid shotgun at Waloonga's feet and waddled after the sled, pigeon-toed in his crotch-high boots.

The little family rode and trotted and hobbled against the worsening north wind, from time to time munching handfuls of snow scooped up from the ground in the way of refreshment, or scraping the rime frost from their eyelashes. Until the dogs wavered and stumbled and the sled ground to a stop.

By then the sunturn was at its darkest.

Ernenek freed the dogs and they started burrowing into the ground and curling up, waiting for the driven snow to blanket them warm. Papik tossed a bit of frozen dog meat into his mouth and, without talking in order to save his breath and also because everybody knew what to do, he started cutting building blocks that Ernenek disposed in a narrowing spiral after the wonted pattern, while Vivi flung snow from outside against the growing wall with a piece of frozen skin, filling the chinks.

The gale was so strong that at times they had to turn their backs to it to catch their breaths before they could proceed.

Ernenek worked slowly, but Papik's blocks also came slowly. The blade he had improvised was less efficient than his broad snow knife that had disappeared at Snow White. But it would do, provided the stifling gale allowed them the time.

It didn't.

Papik had not rested after his return. His furs hadn't had time to dry nor Vivi to mend them. And he hadn't

dropped enough food into his stomach to take the creas-
es out. His mouthful of meat wasn't thawing fast enough
to replace the vanishing energies, and before the igloo
was half up his strength gave out all at once. He
plumped down on his haunches, hanging his head and
wondering whether those who had called him old weren't
right.

Vivi shook him. "Up!" Getting no response she
lashed out: "You call yourself a man?" She spat on his
boots, but in vain. He knew she was trying to warm him,
and that made him smile instead of angry.

"Take off my hides," he mumbled.

"And?"

"Let me die. You two can eat me."

"No." She punched him playfully in the stomach.
"You would be much too tough." She took his knife and
held it out to her son. "Finish the igloo, little one."

But Ernenek stood glaring at her with eyes framed in
rime, stiff and helpless in his store parka.

"What is?" Vivi demanded.

"Somebody's not warm," the boy muttered.

Feeling his face with her cheeks, Vivi discovered that
it was ungreased, the skin dry and tender. The shield of
thick leather grown in many long polar nights had
turned soft and vulnerable by dint of saunas and soap-
ings and indoor heating. Alarm tugged at her stomach.
The frost was winning.

She gripped her son by the shoulders. "Your parents
depend on you, little one. Show them!"

Ernenek couldn't even wrinkle his nose.

She tried to stir his blood by calling him names, a
mere female, no better than a water woman, worse even
than a white man, but she failed again. She made him lie
down on his back then and stretched herself out on top
of him, rubbing his face with hers and breathing her
warmth into his nose. He remained limp and listless.

The cold had made already deep inroads. This wouldn't have occurred only just one brief year ago.

Since she couldn't warm him with anger, she tried it with love.

"Little one," she murmured, "do what a mother wants. And a mother will do anything you'll want."

She hovered over him with her smile, eye to eye and nose to nose, hoping he wouldn't notice her worn teeth in the gloom, but only see her face, beautiful as ever, and more so—softer, warmer. If her bosom hadn't dried up from neglect over the past year, she could have tried warming him with her milk.

After all else had failed, she slipped her bare hand under her son's clothes and caressed his skin, up and down and up and down, whispering:

"Show a mother how a little man becomes a big man."

She kept softly rubbing his nose with hers and breathing into it, cooing and cackling with glee the while; until she had aroused him; until she saw the blood glow in his cheeks and his eyes shine, and she felt him stir. Then she smacked him hard on the hip and got up.

"On your feet, little one! We finish the igloo."

When the shelter stood completed—low and thick and curved, to retain heat and foil the winds—they dragged and pushed Papik in through the tunnel, hung their garments up to thaw, and all huddled together, adding the whelps to fill the surplus space. Whereafter there was nothing left to do but chuckle for having once more dodged death and wait for their bodies to warm up the tight quarters.

All fear and anxiety had vanished. They felt safe and at home in this new igloo, for it was like all their others. The vault, less lofty than a man's head; the tunnel, no wider than a woman's hips; the floor, nowhere longer than a loving couple; no part too large and no part too small, in a miraculous balance between economy and efficiency.

Underfoot, Queen Sedna rocked the ocean to sleep; above, the Air Spirits bolstered the little shelter, adding snow to it.

They could slaughter a dog for the dogs and another for themselves, to recover some strength. Then they would enter hibernation, allowing their body temperatures to drop and sleep to overcome them, so that the fat under their skins might burn but slowly, lasting perhaps until the first seals came out at the crack of spring.

Once they had killed a seal, their survival would be ensured. They would gorge its living flesh until it hung out of their noses and their coursing blood showed in the white of their eyes and tinged in their earlobes. From its bones and frozen meat and any organic matter, including their own, they could make the implements required to get more easily more seals and complete their equipment. They had made it before. It was not impossible that they would make it again.

To tell the full truth, when they surrendered their chilled bodies to the sweetness of sleep, they didn't know whether this wasn't going to be their last igloo.

But they knew that their last igloo would be exactly like this.